NC

RIPPED IN RED

The Pretty Must Die, book 1

By Cynthia Hickey

Written by: Cynthia Hickey
Published by: Winged Publications

ISBN-10:1-944203-02-8
ISBN-13:978-1-944203-02-3

DEDICATION

For all those fans wanting a little spice and a lot of thrill.

PROLOGUE

Twenty-five years earlier

"I'm not interested in going to a frat party." Maureen Monroe opened her beloved copy of *Gone With the Wind* and settled in for a night with her favorite southern belle.

"Stop being a party pooper." Allison lifted her bangs, sprayed them with hairspray, and then attacked the strands with a hair dryer.

Maureen peered over the top of the book. "Why do you want to go anywhere looking like a rooster?"

"It's the style." She grinned. "Blake will be there."

"Still not interested."

"Come on." She faced Maureen. "He's a fox, and definitely interested in you."

"You aren't going to leave me alone, are you?" Maureen sighed and closed her book. "I'm not into the whole college party scene."

“You should have some fun before you graduate and start hunting down the bad guys.”

She groaned and got off her twin bed and headed for the closet. The night was warm, perfect for the new sundress she’d bought from a nearby thrift store. She changed her clothes and pushed Allison away from the mirror. A quick brush of her red hair and a smattering of lipgloss was good enough for her. “I’m ready.”

“That’s it?” Allison pouted. “I hate how pretty you are with so little effort.”

“Good genes.” Maureen slipped her feet into a pair of flat sandals. “Hurry up before I change my mind.” Allison slung a strappy purse over her shoulder and headed out the door, leaving Maureen to follow.

They traipsed across campus to a field on the outskirts where music blared from boom boxes, laughter filled the air, and already drunk frat boys flirted with anything in a skirt. Maureen plastered a smile on her face and headed to the punch bowl.

One sniff told her it was already spiked. She grabbed a glass of water instead and turned to survey the crowd.

“Hey, gorgeous!” Blake slung an arm around her shoulders. “Smile for the camera.”

Someone snapped their picture.

“Come dance with me.”

“You’re drunk.” Whiskey fumes stung her nostrils.

“Not very.” He grabbed her hand and dragged her to a patch of packed down dirt. A slow song started on the radio, and he plastered her against him, leaning heavily on her shoulders.

"Seriously, Blake, I'm not in the mood."

His eyes narrowed. "I'm the envy of every man here."

"So?" She shrugged out of his arms. "There are plenty of pretty girls here dying to dance with you."

"I don't want them." He pouted like a little boy who'd had his favorite toy taken away. "I want you."

"I need to go to the bathroom." She headed for a port-a-potty.

He jogged after her.

As she reached for the handle on the plastic door, he grabbed her hand and dragged her into the bushes. "Blake!"

"I know what will get you in the mood." He nuzzled her neck.

"What have I ever done to give you the impression I'm this type of girl?" She shoved against his chest.

"Plenty," he growled, pushing her farther into the trees.

Before she could scream, she found herself flat on her back in the leaves, something sharp poking her in the thigh. "What's in your pocket?"

"My knife. I don't go anywhere without it," he muttered against her lips. "Relax."

"I'll scream."

He clapped a hand over her mouth. "You can't tease a man the way you do and not expect repercussions."

She bucked under him. Her heart hammered against her chest, her breathing rapid.

He fumbled with the zipper on his jeans, then thrust her dress over her head, shoving part of it into her mouth as a gag.

Whimpering, she continued to fight, struggling to reach the knife in his pocket. Anything to keep him from doing what he planned. She screamed behind the gag as he succeeded, then closed her eyes against the attack. When he collapsed on top of her, she grabbed the knife and slashed, thrusting her dress out of her face.

The knife dug deep into the side of his face.

He howled.

She screamed and rolled him off her, his blood splashing onto her bare arms and chest.

“Hey!” Three college students barged onto the scene.

Blake cupped his torn face. “I’ll kill you.” He pulled up his pants and fled.

Maureen rolled into a ball and sobbed. One of the other men scooped her into his arms. She closed her eyes and gave into the darkness.

1

"Why are you doing this to me?" The beautiful brunette stared up at him with tear-filled eyes.

He tightened the zip tie. "The pretty must die."

"What? Why?" She sobbed. "What are you going to do to me?"

Hadn't his response to her first question told her what was on his mind? Stupidity was one of the reasons he had to kill her...and those like her. The world was filled with people who thought their good looks allowed them to trod over those less attractive and more intelligent. No more! He would rid the world of pretty people, starting with those in Clear Springs, Arkansas.

She kicked at him before he could tie her feet. One of her stilettos clipped his chin, cutting the skin. She struggled to her feet and tottered into the bushes.

He shook his head and swiped the back of his hand across the bleeding cut. She could try to run, but he would catch her. Then, she would pay for all the pain he had experienced in his life.

With a sigh, he pushed to his feet and headed after the woman, grabbing the high heel that had clipped him from the dirt. If she lost the other one, the chase would be more challenging. His heart rate accelerated in anticipation. The victims always ran. His mother had run, then screamed, until he silenced her forever. The only one who hadn't was Maureen. Dear, stupid, teasing Maureen.

His victim's red dress flashed through the trees. She tripped and fell. He lunged forward, grabbing her hair. With one slash of his razor-sharp knife, he rid the world of one more pretty person who thought most people didn't matter. His spirit soared with a hawk circling above the forest.

~

Cassidy Monroe slid her police issued Glock 19 into its holster and rushed out the police department front door. A homicide call warranted quick action before bumbling sightseers ruined the crime scene. "Detective Monroe is headed to the site," she radioed the one and only other officer in Clear Springs: a new man she had yet to meet since he was assigned to their small office that morning after Cassidy's former partner took a job in Little Rock. Before that, she'd worked solo for almost a year. Something she had preferred.

"I'm already here. The body is by the creek. Take the road right past mile marker 59." His deep voice—

was that a Scottish accent?—rippled over the airwaves.

She shook her head and slid behind the wheel of her older model jeep. While she was glad not to be the only officer in their small town, she didn't like being one-upped by the new guy. She set a flashing light in the front window of her vehicle and sped toward the woods. Why did she have to have a partner? In a town as small as Clear Springs, Arkansas, it was quite manageable to work separately.

Twenty minutes later, her jeep bounced down a rutted path barely recognizable as a road. She stopped next to a brand new Ford pickup and cut the ignition. Grabbing her camera and aluminum forensic case, she slid from the jeep and jogged through the trees.

A tall, dark-haired man with eyes the color of a summer sky and a smile that would melt butter, turned to greet her. For the first time in as long as she could remember, she regretted wearing faded jeans and a tee shirt with a small hole under the arm.

"You must be my partner, Cassidy Monroe." He thrust out his hand, his brogue shooting straight to her heart and sending fire through her limbs.

"Yes, and, uh, you are Colin MacKenzie?" She yanked her gaze from his and focused on the body next to the creek. Since when did her smart mouth get tongue-tied?

"Sorry we haven't met before now." Colin squatted next to her. "The call came through before I made it to the office."

"That's fine." Cassidy was at work early every morning and always had her cell phone on for calls that came through during the night.

The body, throat cut, blood soaking into the moss under the victim, was clothed in a scarlet dress. A matching stiletto was placed on a nearby log. Even in death the woman's beauty was easy to see.

"Do we have an ID?" Cassidy snapped a photo, then moved to take one from another angle.

"Yes." Colin motioned to a sequined clutch next to the log. "Amber Wilson, a model from Los Angeles who is here visiting relatives. There are signs of a struggle and evidence to show that she ran from her pursuer. There's something over here that you should see."

Cassidy joined him at the water's edge. Written in the dirt were the words, "The pretty must die."

"That doesn't sound as if our killer will stop with Amber." Her blood chilled.

The only deaths they'd had to deal with in their town prior to this were accidental shootings and car accidents. She wasn't equipped to deal with a serial killer, if this is what they had. She shook her head to clear it. One poor dead woman didn't mean they had a sicko on their hands. It could just as easily have been an angry boyfriend that killed her. "Where's the other shoe?"

"Haven't located it yet."

The sound of voices pulled her from her thoughts. Sarah Robertson, local reporter and all around gossip, teetered toward them on high heels. "Keep her back,"

Cassidy ordered Colin. "She has no sense around a crime scene."

His brow furrowed, no doubt unhappy that she had told him to keep the woman back, but until Cassidy knew what kind of a cop he was, she was remaining in control. Handsome men, in her experience, were most often more worried about how they looked than working hard. Cassidy prided herself on her no-nonsense approach to fashion. Comfortable clothes, gym shoes, and hair pulled back into a ponytail was her daily uniform.

She finished processing the scene as the EMTs arrived. She stood and glanced around to make sure she didn't miss anything important. The area was clean. No footprints. Broken branches that showed the path the victim had fled. No torn fabric or strands of hair on low-hanging branches. Finding the culprit was going to be a challenge.

Colin flirted and kept Sarah occupied, his laugh rumbling across the clearing. Cassidy sighed. She leaned against a tree and waited while the EMTs bagged the body and loaded it onto a portable gurney. Since they knew the victim's identity, the next stop would be to her family. A job Cassidy hated. Their grief always sent her heart spiraling to the pit of her stomach and resulted in her shedding tears into her pillow at night.

"Come on, Don Juan." She motioned for Colin to follow her. "We have work to do."

"Could I get a statement, Detective?" Sarah trotted next to her.

"Didn't Detective MacKenzie tell you anything?" She glanced at Colin.

"No. The man is as handsome as Adonis and as tight-lipped as a clam."

"I can't tell you anything until we notify the family." Cassidy headed for her jeep. "Call me this afternoon."

"Thanks, Cassidy. Bye, Colin," she said in a singsong voice. "You owe me a drink."

Cassidy groaned and climbed into her jeep. "Meet me at the station," she said before closing her door. They might as well ride together from then on out.

~

Working with Cassidy wasn't going to be a hardship. Colin noticed right away that she was thorough and good at her job, not to mention beautiful, despite the plain Jane way she dressed.

He opened the passenger door of her jeep and slid inside. "Would you like me to break the news to the family?"

"I can do it." Her hands trembled as she placed them on the steering wheel.

"I don't mind. I have a degree in psychology."

"Really?" She cast him a surprised look.

"And dual citizenship, not to mention I speak French and Spanish." He grinned. "I'm more than a pretty face."

She rolled her eyes and drove from the parking lot. "Spare me. I'm more interested in your mind and how well you can do your job. It doesn't matter to me what you look like."

He laughed. "You're going to be more fun than my old partner. He was past retirement age, overweight, and more interested in doing paperwork than chasing the bad guys."

"He probably just wanted to live long enough to receive his pension." She glanced at the navigator in her jeep. "You can do the talking with the family."

He nodded and stared out the window, remembering how her amazing green eyes had shadowed over when the subject of visiting the family was broached. It was low on his list of pleasant things to do, but perhaps his offer would soften his new partner's heart toward him. He'd like to be friends with her. He had so few in the States, having left his family behind in Scotland, and turning down a job with Scotland Yard. Killing an innocent young woman would do that to a person.

Funny how life worked. He'd accepted the job in a small Arkansas town to take things easy and found his first case to be a murder. He rubbed his chin, noting he'd forgotten to shave. Life had a strange way of putting a person right smack dab in the middle of something they had no desire to be in.

They stopped in front of a white ranch style house on the outskirts of town. Colin took a deep breath and shoved open his door. What he and Cassidy had to do was nothing compared to what the family would feel.

Taking a deep breath, he rang the doorbell. A middle-aged woman, looking like an older model of the victim, greeted them with a smile.

Colin showed his badge. "May we come in?"

She grabbed her throat, eyes wide, and nodded. "Mark, the police are here."

A thin man, well over six feet tall, a cup of coffee in his hand, joined them in the foyer. "What's my girl done now?"

"Is there somewhere we can sit and talk?" Cassidy asked, stepping next to the wife.

Mrs. Wilson nodded. "This isn't good, is it?"

"No, ma'am." Cassidy took her by the arm and steered her into a modern styled living room.

Once the parents were seated, Colin perched on the sofa next to them. "We'll need a positive identification, but we believe we found Amber's body in the woods. Her identification was close by."

"Drugs?" Mr. Wilson asked, his words shaky.

"No, sir." Colin kept his eyes fixed on the man's, willing strength into him. "She was murdered. I'm so sorry. When was the last time you saw your daughter?"

"Last night. She said she was going to a party," he said. His chin quivered.

"We hated those parties," Mrs. Wilson sobbed. "Once she moved to California to pursue modeling, she got involved in all kinds of things no decent girl should be involved in. Now, she's gone and there is no way she can change her path." She covered her face with her hands.

"Could the things she was involved in have caused someone to kill her?" Colin laid a hand over Mr. Wilson's.

"Here in Clear Springs? I don't see how. The friends she left here are good kids, for the most part."

"But your first statement upon hearing she was dead was to ask if drugs were involved." Colin glanced at Cassidy.

"Some pot. That's all we've ever found her to use here, but out there…in that…place, well, she spent some time in rehab for harder stuff." The pain in the man's eyes was almost Colin's undoing.

He fished a business card from his pocket. "If you think of anything else, anything at all, don't hesitate to call. We'll be back tomorrow to look through her things. Maybe we'll find a clue as to who wanted to harm her. Also, if you could get us a list of her friends here in town, that might help."

Mrs. Wilson nodded. "We'll head to the morgue right away. My poor baby.

Back outside, Cassidy faced Colin. "We should check her room now."

"Let them grieve. We'll be back in the morning."

"What if something is disturbed?" She crossed her arms. "What if they know her murderer and hide evidence?"

"I can sense things about people." He opened the car door for her. "They are nothing more than grieving parents. Let them be. Besides," he grinned, "we have her cell phone. You can spend the next few hours going through her phone log. Come on. We have a killer to catch."

2

"For a pretty girl, she didn't get many calls." Cassidy nursed a cup of coffee while Colin scanned printouts of Amber's phone log.

"How long ago did she leave here?" He peered over the papers. "Maybe she cut her ties so badly no one wanted to remain friends."

Cassidy shrugged. "Maybe." In her experience, the beautiful, popular people were usually surrounded by not-so-true friends. Other than a couple of calls to her modeling agency in California over two weeks ago, Amber's phone was disturbingly empty. "We'll send it to the forensic analyst in Little Rock. They might be able to retrieve something."

"Hmm." Colin leaned back in his chair. "It's possible the killer deleted most of the messages. The question is why?"

"Do you think she was a random target?" Cassidy didn't think so. Instinct told her she knew her killer, at least for a short while before her death. Who in Clear

Springs would want the beautiful dead? Someone tormented by them?

"I don't think so, and I don't think she met that person while she was wearing that red gown, either. I'm still puzzled as to why she had only one shoe. Do you think her killer took the other as a souvenir?" Colin stared out the small office window. "Are there any modeling agencies around here?"

Cassidy shook her head and reached for yesterday's newspaper. "Find someone to get us a copy of every paper printed this week. Maybe our killer placed an advertisement that Amber couldn't resist."

She watched him leave the room. Colin was the epitome of tall, dark, and handsome, towering over her five foot three frame by a foot. His eyes, a starburst of dark and light blue, oh, yes, she had noticed, pierced through to her soul while having the ability to soften and console grieving parents.

What was God thinking to make such a man her partner? Cassidy needed to focus on her job. She glanced at the framed photo of her mother, murdered in cold blood ten years before. She needed to bring her mother's killer to justice. Her case had been cold for too long. Cassidy sighed. She was no closer to solving the death today then she was on her first day as a cop.

"A very distraught mother brought this in." Laura, the over-worked receptionist of the tiny police office set a sheet of lined paper on Cassidy's desk. "She said you were waiting for it."

"Thank you." Cassidy scanned the paper. On it was five names. Written across the top was the heading "Amber's friends". *Thank you, Mrs. Wilson*. At least now they had a place to start.

"Here are the newspapers." Colin dropped them on her desk and leaned over her shoulder.

Her senses went into overdrive at his musky cologne. "Ah, the friends."

"Yes." She handed him the list and reached for a paper, flipping to the classifieds.

On the third paper, Wednesday's edition, she found the first clue to help them solve Amber's murder. "Colin, listen... Needed. A beautiful woman to act as model for evening gown advertisement. Audition in person at ..." She read off the address. "That's a warehouse by the river. Let's go." She grabbed her holster from the back of her chair and dashed from the building, followed closely by Colin.

He snatched the keys from her hand, flashing her a wide smile. "I'll drive."

She rolled her eyes and changed direction to the front passenger seat. It was her jeep. She should be the one driving. "Don't do that again," she said, fastening her seatbelt.

"I don't like being the passenger."

"Neither do I." She glared to show him she meant business, then stared out the window as he drove from the parking lot.

"Don't pout."

She whipped back to face him. "I don't pout."

"Yes, you do."

"Whatever." Having him as her partner was going to be a job in itself. She needed to get him trained, and soon. Her last partner had been more than happy to let her call the shots.

"It looks deserted." Colin cut the ignition.

"It's most likely a dead end, but we have to check it out." Cassidy unholstered her weapon and pushed open her door.

"I'll enter first." Colin held out his hand. "Please."

She stared into his face, noting a shadow of pain flicker across his eyes. Chivalry, and something else, was alive and well in Arkansas.

Guns held at the ready, they approached a metal door to the side of a larger rolling door. Cassidy gave Colin a nod as he turned the door handle. The door swung open with a groan.

Colin took a deep breath and stepped in. Cassidy followed, then moved to his side.

As suspected, the warehouse was devoid of life. Their footsteps echoed in the cavernous room. In a far corner draped a curtain. A tripod lay on its side. The type of lights used by photographers were placed around the photography area. Footprints marred the dust.

Cassidy squinted, making out something pinned to the backdrop. She moved closer. A photo of a smiling, posing Amber wearing the dress they'd found her in was taped there. The killer had lured the girl here, then taken her to the woods and murdered her. "I doubt he'll use this place again."

"You think he plans on killing again?" Colin slid his gun into its holster.

"I know he will." She reached a trembling hand toward the photo. "I've seen his setup before."

He narrowed his eyes. "Explain."

"This is the same man that murdered my mother."

In the case files were crime scene photos of this exact scene, but in a different location. Always beautiful, Cassidy's mother had gone undercover as a model to catch a man who preyed on women who loved the camera. He'd never been caught.

~

"I'll get your bag out of the car. We need to process the scene." Colin jogged outside, giving Cassidy a few minutes to compose herself. He had a lot of questions that needed answers, but they would wait. He pulled her aluminum case from the trunk. By the time he joined her, she stood ramrod straight, her features composed.

She took the case from him and got to work. Colin was perceptive if nothing else. She still needed time. He was fine with it.

While she snapped pictures of the scene, he squatted next to the footprints. They weren't looking for a small man. The prints were as large as the ones Colin left, putting the unsub at six feet tall, at least. He'd read Cassidy's file. He was familiar with her mother's case. How had the murderer escaped capture for so many years?

He straightened. "Do you think that perhaps the unsub doesn't live in Clear Springs? Maybe he returns for an anniversary of some kind."

Cassidy glanced his way. "Since my mother, we haven't had anything like this happen again until now. That was ten years ago."

"There has to be a trigger. A killer doesn't stay dormant for ten years, then kill again unless something pulled him out." He stared at Cassidy. "You just had a birthday."

"Yeah, so?" She slid her camera back in her case, then jerked upright. "I'm the same age my mother was when she died. You think I'm the trigger? The target?"

He scanned the loose pants and baggy blouse she wore. "You're beautiful enough, but other than that, you don't fit the profile of his victims. That's why you downplay your looks. Because your mother was killed for hers."

"How I dress is no concern of yours." She headed for the door.

"I'm right, aren't I?" He moved in front of her.

"Move." She shoved past him. Her actions were answer enough.

Colin strung crime scene tape across the warehouse entrances before joining Cassidy at the jeep. He wanted to press for information; make her see he was right. And, if he was, she was in grave danger. The killer could be coming after her.

She slid behind the steering wheel and gave him a defiant look. Fine, he'd let her drive, but they were not finished with their discussion.

"Let's grab something to eat before visiting the people on the friends list."

"A burger okay?"

"Sounds great." He settled in and kept his mouth shut for the next fifteen minutes. They would be spending a lot of time together. He'd get the answers he wanted...in time.

"Bill's has the best burgers." Cassidy stopped in front of a barn-like building.

Colin's stomach rumbled. Dives usually had the best food, and he'd skipped breakfast. He slid from the jeep and held the diner door open. Once Cassidy was relaxed with good food, he'd grill her for more information. If she remained tight-lipped, he'd spend some more time immersed in her mother's cold case.

A waitress led them to a booth in front of a large plate-glass window. Colin waited until Cassidy was seated, then slid across from her. He pretended to peruse the menu when he actually studied her.

The vibrant red hair, dark green eyes, straight nose and full lips. Even without makeup and her hair sloppily piled on top of her head, she was stunning. If she were the target, why had the unsub killed Amber? Why not go after Cassidy years ago after killing her mother?

"You know the unsub." He dropped the menu on the table.

She sighed. "I've thought so, too, but can't think of a single person who wanted my mother dead." She shook her head. "She went undercover to find the person killng models. That's where she met him. I don't think he's a family friend."

"Did you meet anyone new while she was undercover?"

"I don't think so. I was fifteen years old." She raised cold eyes to him. "I have no idea whether my mother brought her work home with her. There wasn't a parade of men coming through our home."

He held up his hands in defense. "I'm sorry. That's not what I meant at all."

"I didn't take unnecessary offense." She stiffened. "Mom never brought anyone home. She said all she needed was me and her job. I don't think I've met the killer."

The waitress arrived to take their orders, thus giving him a few moments to rethink his direction of questioning. After they both ordered cheeseburger meals, he rested his arms on the table and kept his gaze locked on Cassidy's face. His best intense stare usually worked on those he questioned.

Cassidy rolled her eyes. "Cut it out. I can give that look with the best of them."

He laughed and straightened. "I'm only trying to help you. It's quite possible that, by solving Amber's murder, we also solve your mother's."

"That would be convenient."

"You're a prickly gal, aren't you? I'm not the enemy, you know."

She sighed. "I'm sorry. I spent three years of my life in foster care. I don't trust easily."

"And I come across a bit strong."

"A bit." Her eyes softened, the corners of her mouth easing into a smile. "I'll try and think harder about who I might know. That's all I can promise."

"That's all I ask. That you don't discount the possibility that your mother angered someone badly enough that they would resurface, and possibly be coming after you."

~

He stared at the ten faces in front of him and smiled. Not one of them could be considered goodlooking. One or two mildly attractive, maybe. All had responded to his post on a hard-to-find chat room and a personal ad in the newspaper about being mistreated by those whom society looked upon favorably. After a period of testing, he would find his worthy followers. Outcasts willing to help him in his quest.

"All of those who have ridiculed us, beaten us down, bullied us because they deem themselves better than us based upon our looks must be dealt with." He ran a finger down the scar that ran from his right eye to his mouth. "They must pay for their crimes against us. If you do not have the stomach for revenge, you are free to go. Now."

One man, slight in build, stood. "I thought this was a support group. Sorry, but this isn't for me." He glanced around the room. "May God have mercy on all of you." He spun and almost ran from the room.

Draco, the name he had given himself, the name for Dragon, laughed. The man had made his choice and would be dealt with later. The dragon left no witnesses. Made no excuses for his plans. He definitely didn't call upon a God who had cursed him in love.

"Is there anyone else who feels that my quest is unjust? Is there anyone else willing to remain in the shadow of conceit and be stomped upon? If so, leave now. Once you begin your training, the only way out is through the fire of my wrath. I have designed special coats with colors of protection once you have proven yourselves worthy." He motioned to leather jackets hanging on the wall. "There is a gold bowl on the stand in front of me. Write on slips of paper all those who have wronged you and they will be dealt with. Everything you need to start over afterward is in the packet under your seat."

The remaining nine, seven men and two women, stayed seated, their faces a mixture of hope and the desire for revenge. Once Draco finished with them, they would all want those who had tormented them to die, and he would help them. They would love him. He would become their hero.

3

Cassidy poured coffee from the pitcher into a mug and handed it to Colin. If they started pursuing the track of the unsub being the same person who murdered her mother, they might miss a clue leading to who killed Amber. She couldn't risk that. The poor girl deserved justice. Still, the lure of finding her mother's killer...

"I can practically see the wheels turning in your head." Colin leaned back in his chair and propped his feet on the desk. "Want to talk about it?"

"No." Cassidy took her seat and rifled through the few envelopes on her desk. With her and Colin as the only two police officers in town, some days the mail piled up. She'd once tried to have the receptionist wade through it, but some of the darker "fan" mail they received sent the poor woman into fits.

She spotted a plain white envelope with the address being glued on letters from a magazine. "Got something."

After pulling on a pair of rubber gloves, she slit the envelope with a letter opener. "It's a poem" The yellowed page signified the sender had ripped it from an old book.

BY LORD BYRON

Colin peered over her shoulder. "He has seen through your attempts to hide how attractive you are."

"I'm not hiding anything." She slid the page into a bag and yanked off her gloves. "I simply find it easier to wear comfortable clothes and have a non-fussy hairstyle."

"No, you're definitely hiding." He perched on the corner of her desk. "Now, me...I choose to embrace my handsomeness." A dimple winked near the right corner of his mouth. "People tend to talk to those who make an effort."

Cassidy rolled her eyes and tore her gaze away from lips that looked as if they would kiss with little provocation. She didn't scare easily, but ice ran through her veins. Would the unsub come after her or was the poem nothing more than a note from an admirer? Could it be that the killer admired Cassidy's way of downplaying her looks or was he toying with her?

Yes, she tried to hide how pretty she was, despite her saying otherwise. Beauty had gotten her mother killed. Now, possibly the same man was bent on erasing more beautiful women from the earth.

Downplaying her looks helped her get the job done. She definitely didn't need the distraction of admiring glances from men while women were dying.

"We need to send this to the lab in Little Rock." She handed the bag containing the poem to Colin. "I doubt they'll find anything, but we can always hope."

Something that seemed in short supply lately. Hope. It had done nothing for her mother, a devout churchgoer, nor Cassidy's father who had died when she was too young to remember him. The song phrase that only the good die young ran through her head.

The phone rang. She answered it as Colin left the room. "Officer Monroe."

"Detective?" Laura's voice wavered. "You have a call on line one. Some hikers found another body."

"Thank you, Laura. I'll take it."

She pressed the button on the phone for line one. "Officer Monroe." She listened as a very excited woman explained how she and her girlfriend were hiking and stumbled across a woman tied to a tree. Hanging up, Cassidy grabbed her shoulder holster and dashed off to find her partner.

"Colin, we've got another one." She raced past where he leaned over the receptionist desk, flirting as usual. What would it be like to be so sure of oneself? By the time he joined her, she was behind the wheel of her jeep with the engine running.

He slid into the passenger seat and clicked his seatbelt into place. "You know, my truck is newer." He raised his eyebrows. "Another one in two days?"

"We don't know it's the same guy." She turned onto Main Street and headed for the popular hiking trail on the mountain. "And I prefer my jeep."

He shrugged. "Not yet, but we'll see that it is."

"Are you always this sure of yourself?"

"Always." He cut her a sideways glance.

She wished she were. Cassidy was a good detective, she'd been told so many times, but still that niggling in the back of her mind told her she wasn't good enough. Not good enough for her mother to stay alive, not good enough to have found a permanent family after her death, and now...what if she weren't good enough to catch a potential serial killer?

She parked the jeep alongside the hiking trail and cast a glance at two hysterical women who approached at a run. She took a step back.

"I'll take care of this." Colin grinned and motioned for the women to step beside the jeep.

"Thank you." Calming distraught people was not anywhere close to the top of things Cassidy was good at. She opened the back of the jeep and grabbed her crime scene case.

With one last look at Colin, who had managed to find bottles of water somewhere and offered them to the women, she headed down the trail. Sunlight filtered through tree tops, giving the illusion of a perfect autumn day. The body tied to a tree belied that fact.

"Lizzie Borden took an ax." Cassidy pulled on a pair of gloves, then placed a number beside the bloody murder weapon and snapped a photo before turning back to the victim. "And gave her mother forty whacks."

While the first victim had her throat slit, this one had taken many whacks of an ax to her head and torso almost rendering her features unrecognizable. She shook her head and squatted next to a beaded red purse that matched the woman's gown. If not for the red clothing, she might have thought they were dealing with another perpetrator.

She rifled through the evening purse and pulled out the woman's driver's license. "Pretty. Samantha Meyers" Of course, she would be. Someone wanted all the pretty people dead. The poor girl was nineteen years old and from Oklahoma. What was she doing on a mountain top in Arkansas?

"And when she saw what she had done, she gave her father forty-one."

"Nursery rhymes?" Colin squatted next to her.

"Came to mind when I entered the crime scene." Cassidy handed him the license. "See if you can find out if anyone in Lawton reported this poor girl missing." She straightened and scanned the scene. Something didn't make sense. Why slit one girl's throat and go to such extremes with this one?

"This girl was reported missing yesterday." Colin snapped his cell phone closed. "She disappeared from a party." He glanced around the area. "What are you thinking?"

"That we're dealing with more than one killer."

"Hmm." He stared into the trees. "It's possible. But what would be the motivation?"

"That's what we need to figure out." She sighed. "It's time to bring in the FBI."

He groaned. "They'll take over."

"True, but we need all the help we can get." She dug out her cell phone as the ambulance arrived, sirens wailing. "What about the two who found her?"

"They're waiting for us at the station. I hope you don't mind that I put a case of bottled water in the backseat this morning. If we're going to be taking your car most of the time—"

She waved off his explanation. "It came in handy." She placed a call to the FBI, explaining the two murders, then hung up. "They'll get back to us later."

~

Draco watched from a thick stand of trees as the one he loved and admired found his latest gift to her. Not that Draco personally killed the woman, no, not this one, but he had guided his prodigy. Too bad the silly woman had gone so far overboard in her killing. Still, practice made perfect. Her motive had been warranted.

One day, the pretty people of the world would learn that treating those less attractive with scorn and rudeness had terrible consequences. Someday, they would bow before Draco and his kind. He traced the scar on his face with his forefinger. Just as his love had done minutes before her death. Tears and pleas didn't work to sway one as powerful as he.

The object of his desire turned and stared in his direction. Not that she could see him until he willed it, but he melted further into the shadows, freeing the tail of his shirt from the eager clutches of a bush. Their day would come.

~

Back at the office, Colin tapped a pencil on his desk and stared at the case board. Two deaths in two days. Both beautiful women in red evening gowns. No suspects. He studied his partner.

Cassidy had stood for ten minutes, staring at the board, unmoving, as if she could will a clue to be there that wasn't. He'd read her file. He knew how good she was at what she did, but this time...they were in over their heads.

He straightened and stopped tapping as three agents, all in dark suits, entered the tiny office. The tallest, a large African American, approached Colin. "I'm Agent Ingram, these are Agents Smith and Weston. No wisecracks, please."

Colin stood and shook his hand. "Wouldn't think of it. I'm Detective Colin MacKenzie and this is Detective Cassidy Monroe, head detective on the case."

Cassidy turned, gave them a nod, and resumed studying the board. "I'm guessing you will want to move to the conference room? It isn't much larger, but we can squeeze in."

Agent Ingram returned her nod. "Are you the Colin MacKenzie that turned down working for the FBI?"

"One and the same." Colin took a deep breath.

Cassidy turned and stared.

He shrugged. "I prefer to dabble in computers in my spare time. Pounding the pavements is more my style." When the FBI asked him to sit at a desk all day and search for cyber crime he had turned them down. Sure, he still searched the internet on his off hours, sometimes sending something suspicious their way, but that type of life wasn't for him.

"Our loss." Ingram motioned his head to the door. "Shall we?"

The other two agents wheeled the case board into the conference room, placing it against a far wall. Once everyone was inside, Cassidy told them of what had transpired over the last two days and her's and Colin's suspicions that they were looking at more than one killer.

Ingram nodded several times during Cassidy's speech. "Agent Weston will provide a press release and make a statement to the press. We'll notify the Lawton police and visit the latest victim's family."

Cassidy crossed her arms. "I do hope you will continue to let us investigate."

"Of course. You've had direct contact from the unsub. We'll keep all channels of communication open and will ask that you do the same. In fact, we insist the two of you follow any leads you may have." With a thin-lipped smile, the three agents left the room.

Follow the leads. He knew darn well they didn't have any. He was amusing himself with the fact Colin chose to hit the streets rather than work for the FBI. He met Cassidy's stern gaze. "Where to?"

"I want to revisit the crime scene. I feel like we're missing something." She grabbed a black hoodie from the back of a chair. "When we were out there before, I felt like we were being watched."

Colin froze mid-stride. "You think the unsub was there?"

"Not sure. It could be nothing more than the heebie jeebies from a dead body, but I'd still like to take a look."

Colin wasn't going to disregard her intuition. Life had taught him to listen to a woman's gut feeling. He dashed into their office long enough to grab a light jacket from the back of his chair and rushed to meet Cassidy at the jeep.

Rain fell in a steady stream, the autumn day dark and drab. Fitting for a murder scene. He clicked his seat belt into place and listened to the steady thump of the wiper blades. He almost requested they wait until the next day to search the woods, but if the rain continued for too long, any signs could be washed away. They couldn't take that chance.

"Why didn't you tell me you turned down the FBI?" Cassidy cut him a sideways glance.

"It was in my file."

"I didn't read your file."

"Maybe you should have." He quirked his mouth. "I read every page of yours."

She frowned. "Good for you." She turned down the road that led to the hiking trail. When they stopped, she grabbed her camera and case from the trunk, and headed into the trees.

Yellow crime scene tape sagged under the increasing rain. After slipping a protective cover over her phone, Cassidy pulled up her hood. She stepped to the edge of the crime scene and looked to her left.

"There," she said. "Earlier, I thought I heard something."

Colin unlatched his gun. "Let's take a closer look."

Shaking the rain from his hair, he led the way in the direction she pointed. He stopped a few feet into a thick stand of trees. "Someone stood here." He squatted. "See the prints? Looks like a size eleven gym shoe." Why hadn't she said something earlier?

"Here is a scrap of fabric. Could be from our unsub."

Colin stood. "If you thought someone was watching, why didn't you say anything?"

"I wasn't sure. It wasn't until I thought more about it that I remembered." She snapped a picture of the fabric on the branch, then used tweezers to pull it free. She dropped it into a small bag. "At first, I thought it nothing more than nerves."

"You've got good instincts, Cassidy. Trust them." He placed his foot beside the print while Cassidy took a picture. "Even if nothing pans out, go with every gut feeling."

"I usually do." She placed her camera and the scrap of fabric into her case. "A second murder in two days rattled me a bit. I'm focused now."

"It was the poem, not the dead body that threw you off kilter."

"Think what you want."

She sure was a prickly woman. As beautiful as the landscape of Scotland and as sharp as a thorn bush. He'd break through her defenses, eventually. He had to. They had to be able to trust each other. But, he had a feeling his partner trusted very few people.

He gave the area another quick scan, hoping they hadn't missed anything else. When the killer struck again, and Colin knew he, or she, would, he'd keep a sharp eye on their surroundings. If he showed up at one crime scene, he'd show up at another.

What was he looking for? Why hadn't he taken a shot at the officers? Did he get off on watching reactions to his deed? Possibly, but Colin thought it might be deeper than that. After the poem Cassidy received, he had a sinking feeling that the women might be some kind of sick, twisted gift for his partner.

4

Cassidy tossed her keys in the bowl on the foyer table and headed to the kitchen. Nothing ended a day on the job more than a glass of wine and a bowl of popcorn. She sipped her Moscato while she waited for the microwave to signal her meal was ready.

She'd messed up. When they'd examined the body that morning, and she'd felt eyes watching her, she should have investigated then, and not chalked it up to nerves and an over-active imagination. They'd lost valuable time. If she had taken her feeling to heart, the killer might be behind bars right that moment.

The microwave dinged, and she withdrew her supper. Maybe not the most nutritious meal, but it was her favorite. Popcorn and a drink was what she needed after the last two days.

She moved to the living room and turned on the television. Agent Weston stood behind a podium, alerting the town and surrounding areas to the possibility of a serial killer in their midst. She was good, telling them what they needed to know, but not giving so much information that she jeopardized the investigation.

Cassidy sat on the sofa and balanced the bowl of popcorn on her lap. Colin could have been one of the agents in charge. Why be content to work for a small town police force? Cassidy would give her eye teeth for an FBI offer. Her partner was definitely an enigma. Just when she thought she had him figured out, he surprised her. It seemed Colin MacKenzie might be more than a handsome face and a killer smile. Too bad she only wanted to know enough about him to work with him.

Popcorn and glass of wine finished, she turned off the television and climbed the stairs to her room. She placed her holster and gun on the bed, then whipped off her shirt. She froze. The closet door was open about two inches. Meticulous to a fault, Cassidy had a place for everything in her house and never left doors open that were meant to be closed.

She slowly slid her weapon from its holster. Mouth as dry as desert sand, she soft-footed her way to the closet and whipped the door open. Empty, except for jeans, tee shirts, and her few dressier items of clothing. She turned a slow circle in her room. Nothing seemed out of place. Her few pieces of jewelry rested in a crystal candy dish on the dresser. The latest crime novel she was reading sat on the nightstand.

She moved to the bathroom. Towels hung straight, hygiene products in place. Had she been so preoccupied with yesterday's murder that she hadn't noticed her open closet? There was a first time for everything, her old partner used to say. Still, the fact that something seemed off wouldn't leave her. She wouldn't brush it off as she had that morning. Instead, she did a thorough sweep of her home…and found nothing amiss.

There was no other explanation. She was getting sloppy.

Back in her room, she flopped across the bed and stared at the ceiling. She had to have left the closet door open. Her windows were locked, so were her doors. Had her mind been so consumed with the case that she'd forgotten parts of her morning routine?

Ugh. She got up and headed for the bathroom. After turning on the water, she got undressed, dropping her clothes on the floor. She reached over and closed and locked the bathroom door. If someone had gotten into her house, she definitely didn't want to be caught naked.

Her cell phone rang from the nightstand in the bedroom. They could leave a message. She stepped under the hot spray of the faucet and closed her eyes. A big mistake. The faces of the two victims swam across her eyelids.

What if the man who killed them really was the same one who had taken her mother's life? Was it possible that after all these years, her mother's case would finally be solved?

She lathered her hair and turned her back to the faucet. Was Colin right and the perp was fixated on Cassidy? Why? She didn't fit the profile of the victims.

Well, not in her day-to-day life. If she dressed nice and put on makeup, she would be just as pretty. She rinsed and turned off the water. Others in law enforcement wouldn't take her seriously if she looked like a Barbie doll.

Still…a momentary thought of luring the perp from hiding by upping her looks flitted across her mind and was quickly dismissed. Jeans and sweatpants were better suited for a law officer in the small town of Clear Springs.

Her cell phone rang again. She sighed, wrapped a towel around her, and hurried to answer it. The caller hung up before she could press the button.

"Why aren't you answering your phone?"

She grabbed her gun and whirled, keeping a tight hold of her towel. "Colin! I could have shot you." She narrowed her eyes. "How did you get in here?"

"I picked your lock." He leaned against the doorjamb, looking as delicious as a slice of chocolate cake. "You don't have a very good security system."

"Why are you here?" She set her gun back on the stand and headed for the bathroom.

"You didn't answer your phone."

She rolled her eyes and slammed the door. Of all the nerve. A smile teased at her lips. The wide-eyed look on his face at seeing her in nothing but a towel almost made her forget her anger. Almost. Darn. She'd forgotten to grab clothes.

She opened the door an inch. "Could you hand me those clothes over the back of the chair, please?"

"You sleep in gym shorts?" He squeezed them through the crack in the door. "Not very sexy."

"No one to impress." She quickly got dressed and ran a brush through her hair. She stepped out of the bathroom and glared. "Explain again why you're here?"

"Oh." He pulled a folded sheet of paper from his pocket. "I was doing some computer searching and ran across this website you might be interested in. Mind if I use your computer?"

"In here." She led him to the second bedroom which she used as a guest room, not that she ever had any guests, and an office. She flipped the top of the laptop and stepped aside.

Colin's fingers flew across the keyboard. What he pulled up make her stomach roll.

"How did you find this?" She watched in horror as the first victim, Amber Wilson, dashed through the forest, glancing with terror over her shoulder. The video went on to film her killer slash her throat.

"Here's the other one." Colin clicked to another link.

"My God." Cassidy's knees sagged. "Snuff films."

He nodded. "I'm not convinced the films are the reason for the murders, but merely a convenient means to let others enjoy the unsub's handiwork."

She leaned against the desk and put a hand over her face. Not once in her years as a detective had she seen something so sick.

Colin grabbed her by the shoulders and yanked her to him. Before she could take a breath, his head descended, his lips claiming hers.

For a second, she responded, before stepping back and stomping on his foot. "What are you doing?"

"Ow." He grabbed his foot and grinned. "I thought you were going to faint. Kissing you was the first thing I could think of."

~

Her lips were as soft and sweet as he thought they'd be. And, for a moment, she'd melted and returned his kiss. His partner wasn't as made of ice as she pretended to be.

"Don't do that again." She poked his chest with her finger.

"No promises." He motioned back to the laptop. "Now that that's out of the way, any ideas how you want to handle this?"

She shook her head. "What made you think to look for these videos?"

"I couldn't sleep. I kept feeling as if there was something we were missing, so I started playing around. If I were a killer, proud enough of my handiwork to send the detective in charge a love poem, what would I do?" He rubbed his hands down his face. "It's disgusting how my mind works sometimes."

"Can we get a trace?"

"I've already notified the FBI agents. Hopefully, they can do more on their end."

"Can we close down the site?"

"Sure, but the killer will just open a new one." He grabbed her elbow. "Let's get something to eat."

"I had popcorn." She yanked free.

"That's not dinner."

"How can you eat after watching that?"

"I'm a healthy male with a clear conscience." Mostly, anyway. "Let's grab a burger."

"Fine. Give me a minute."

He watched as she made sure her closet was closed, checked under her bed, and then made the rounds of the house checking doors and windows. She was thorough. He shook his head at her OCD tendency and held the front door open for her to go ahead of him. "You really need to update your security. I know a guy."

"I'm sure you do." She slid behind the wheel of her jeep and smiled through the window.

Colin laughed and dashed through a lightly falling rain to the passenger side. Working with Cassidy promised to be fun. "You'll have to let me drive sometime," he said, sliding into the jeep.

"You can try if I'm ever incapable." She turned the ignition and backed from the drive. "I know just the place for good barbeque where they won't mind that I'm dressed like a teenage boy."

A sexy teenager, but he wisely kept his mouth shut. They remained silent until she turned into a burger joint with outdoor seating. The smell of roasting beef teased his growling stomach. He loved dive places. They often served the best food.

"I'll order," Cassidy said, sliding from the jeep. "Double bacon cheeseburgers with seasoned fries and lots of sauce. You'll love it. Want a beer?"

"Yeah." He followed her, pulling out his wallet. A man never let a woman pay for dinner. At least not this man. He slid his money through the order window before Cassidy was finished giving their selection.

"Feeling emasculated?" She quirked an eyebrow.

"Not anymore." He grinned and sat at a table for two under the red and white striped awning. The night was cool, but the view in front of him was hot.

Long shapely legs under sagging shorts. A too-big-for-her tee shirt, and a cascade of red hair. Even dressed as she was, Cassidy was definitely the most beautiful woman he'd ever seen. He was one lucky Scot.

Her amazing emerald eyes narrowed as she approached the table. "Are you laughing at me?"

"Admiring the view."

"Right." She shook her head as she took her seat.

"You seemed jumpy when I got to your house." He folded his arms on the table. "Mind telling me why? Don't say it's because I surprised you. You weren't that surprised to see someone in your house. Why?"

She sighed. "My closet door was open when I got home."

He pressed his lips together to keep from smiling. "That's it?"

"I never leave it open. You saw me prepare to leave tonight."

True. She had checked her closet and made sure it was closed tight. "Did you sweep the place?"

"Yes." She shrugged. "I'm sure I was preoccupied this morning."

"Don't brush it off." He'd make sure he checked her home before leaving for the night. It could be nothing, but with the type of person they were dealing with, he wasn't taking any chances. From the stern look on Cassidy's face, she wasn't either, no matter how inconsequential she tried to make things look.

"May I take a look at the case board on your mother's murder?" He asked as a young man brought their food. "I know you have one."

Her gaze could cut steel. "Why?"

"Maybe I'll catch something you've missed."

"I haven't missed anything." She pointed a french fry in his direction. "Now that we suspect she was killed by the same man who killed these women, I'll take a deeper look."

"It can't hurt to have two sets of eyes going over it." He bit into beefy heaven. Bacon grease mixed with cheese on top of a well-cooked burger and a homemade bun. "This is wonderful."

"I come here a couple of times a week."

"I can see why. What's our plan for tomorrow?"

"The morgue. Maybe the medical examiner can tell us something new." She dipped her fry into an orangish sauce. "We've got to get a break soon, or this case will join the cold case files."

He put his hand over hers. "We'll catch this guy. Have faith. My guess is...he'll come to us."

~

Draco watched from his parked car as the detectives enjoyed their food. He'd followed them from Cassidy's home, pleased to see that the man hadn't stayed long and Cassidy left wearing the least sexy and revealing item in her closet. Still, those were her nightclothes. She needed to be careful. Any infraction with the Scot would result in serious consequences. She belonged to Draco. No one else. One day, she would realize this.

He lowered his binoculars, still able to see them clearly, even though Cassidy's gorgeous features were a bit blurred by the rain. The bible said that a woman's beauty should come from within. Her's radiated so brightly, it dimmed the sun. She was truly a jewel among women. Just as her mother had been, before succumbing to the lure of vanity.

His cell phone vibrated in his pocket. Mary Jones. Her killing of the first woman on her list had been sloppy. No finesse. "Yes?"

"When can I do the other one?"

"You need some training, Mary."

"I know I got carried away. It won't happen again." Her smoker's voice rattled, grating on his nerves.

"Perhaps, you can practice on Harold."

"The man who left the first meeting? I don't have anything against him."

"He'll talk. Do you want to go to jail?"

"I don't care. I have nothing. But, I'd at least like to take care of my ungrateful step-sisters first. Fine. What do you want me to do?"

"Make yourself as presentable as possible and lure dear Harold to me. I'll take you through it step-by-step." He hung up before she could argue further. Poor Mary was going to be a trial. Draco expected unquestioning obedience. Something she lacked. After one more look through the binoculars at his heart's desire, he turned the key in the ignition of his jeep and drove home, twirling the pair of black satin panties he'd stolen from Cassidy's drawer on his finger.

5

Cassidy slathered Vicks under her nose, gave Colin a wry smile, and then pushed open the door to the morgue housed in the hospital of a neighboring town. The smell under her nose didn't quite mask the odor coming from the examining table in front of her, but it helped.

Olivia Sparrow, the medical examiner, looked up with a grim expression. "Nasty."

No argument there. "What can you tell us?"

"I don't think these women were killed by the same perp." She pulled the sheet from the first victim. "Here, the throat was slit with one deep slash. A strong person." She moved to the other girl. "This one...some of the axe marks aren't deep...more like the attacker was tiring."

Cassidy stepped aside as Colin leaned in for a closer look. "Any evidence on the perp?"

"No fibers, if that's what you're asking." Olivia shook her head. "Other than threads from the gown she wore. But…" she grinned. "We do have a partial print from the button on Amber Wilson's gown." She handed a sheet of paper to Cassidy. "I've already sent it to forensics."

"I doubt he's in the system, but good job." She folded the paper and put it in her pocket.

"Look." Colin pointed to drops on Amber's ankle. "This her blood?"

"I haven't checked." Olivia withdrew a cotton swab from a nearby jar and took a sample of the blood. "It could be."

Colin straightened. "Or, we could have gotten a break."

Like the fingerprint, Cassidy doubted the killer's DNA was on file. But, if he was the one who killed her mother, the print would prove it. They'd found a partial on the scene then, too. Almost as if the killer left them bread crumbs, then swept everything away when the cops got too close. She'd make a phone call once she returned to the precinct. If it was the same man, then she'd let Colin look at the case board on her mother's murder.

For the first time in years, hope sprang anew. Maybe Cassidy could finally get the justice she'd been seeking.

She grabbed a tissue from a nearby box and wiped the Vicks from her upper lip on the way out the door. "I want to see whether this print is in the database or not. We can do that from the office."

"What do you think about the ME's opinion on multiple unsubs?" Colin held her jeep door open for her.

"I think Olivia is correct." She slid into the driver's seat and waited until Colin got in before speaking again. "My gut tells me the crimes are related, but I haven't put together how. I also want to check the newspaper again and see whether another ad coincided with the second victim."

"I can look for that while you search for the print." Colin clicked his seatbelt into place. "We'll catch this guy."

"There are no guarantees." She drove down the freeway toward town.

Hopefully, Colin was right. Cassidy hated being a pessimist, but life had taught her to never get her hopes too high. When she did, something dashed them into a million pieces. Every time.

She parked in front of the police station and headed inside, leaving Colin to follow. She needed to know without a doubt whether the print found on Amber's dress matched the one at the scene of her mother's murder.

At her desk, she booted up her computer and scanned in the print. While she waited, she chewed the cuticle on her left thumb.

Finally. The print came back as a match. Still no name in the system, but it was definitely the same killer.

She slumped in her chair. "It's the same."

Colin raised an eyebrow. “As your mother’s killer?”

“Yes.” She ducked her head before he saw the tears in her eyes. She’d waited so long for a break in her mother’s case. “I’ll show you the case board now.”

~

Colin followed Cassidy into her basement. Against one wall hung a giant chalkboard. He maneuvered through stacks of boxes to get closer.

She swiveled the board to show photos, post it notes, and index cards placed in chronological order. “I’ve done everything I can to keep up with what was happening before the case was closed. Until today, I had nothing new to add in a very long time.” She wrote “prints from Amber Wilson match prints found next to Maureen Monroe” on an index card and tacked it to the corkboard.

“You’ve managed to collect quite a bit.” He peered at the photo of her mother in a royal blue gown. Her throat was slit the same as Amber Wilson. And, like the younger woman, she was quite beautiful. Cassidy was almost a dead ringer for her mother. “You said you grew up in foster care. Where’s your father?”

“Mom never told me about him, no matter how many times I asked.”

“She was young when she had you.”

“Nineteen, almost twenty.” Cassidy leaned against a folding table. “I didn’t pry. It was clear the subject of my father hurt her to talk about.”

“Hmm.” He turned and scanned the crowded basement. Most of the boxes were marked as her mother's things. "I think we should start another case board for Amber and Samantha. Keep it close by and compare with your mother's. I think there will be a lot of overlapping."

"Did you find anything in the newspaper?"

"Yep. Another advertisement for modeling. I've asked for a paper to be on my desk first thing every morning." He motioned with his head for her to follow him upstairs. They'd headed straight for the basement upon arriving. "Go through your house and see if anything is out of place." He still thought Cassidy was the killer's target this time around. If he didn't plan on killing her, he had something else planned. It wouldn't hurt to search the house for bugs, then install a better security system no matter how against such measures she was.

He followed her around the downstairs and then up to her bedroom. The closet door was ajar.

"I know I closed it this morning. I was extra careful after yesterday." She moved to close it.

"Wait." He pulled his weapon from his shoulder holster. "Let me check out the closet. You look around the rest of the room."

He opened the door enough to step inside the small walk-in. Clothes filled half the space, confirming that Cassidy wasn't like other women. All the women he knew had jammed closets.

A few shoeboxes and a small safe occupied the top shelf. There. Tucked into the corner was a small hole. As his gaze locked on the camera, he heard a soft hiss. He held his breath too late and toppled to the floor.

When he woke, Cassidy bent over him. Her eyes clouded with worry. "What happened?" she asked.

"There's a camera in the corner and some sort of gas released." He forced himself to cough and crawled out of the closet. "I'm calling my security friend."

"Why didn't the gas release this morning when I got dressed?" She grabbed his arm and helped him to his feet.

"He doesn't want to harm you…yet." He sat on the edge of her bed and cradled his pounding head in his hands. "I held my breath as soon as I heard the release. I'll be fine." If he hadn't been paying attention, he could be dead.

"You need to go to the hospital."

"If I'm not dead now, the gas isn't going to kill me." He dug his cell phone from his pocket and dialed his friend. After getting assurance he'd be there within the hour, Colin held a finger to his lips, then whispered. "No talking until the house is checked out."

"Then, at least lay down." She tried to push him back on the bed.

"Not alone." He winked.

"For crying out loud, Colin! Now is not the time to be a flirt." She rolled her eyes. "You could have died."

"But, I didn't. A drink of water would be nice, though." Anything to wash the bitter taste out of his throat.

"I'll be right back." She ducked into the bathroom.

Colin stared at the closet. The fact the gas released when Colin entered the closet told him a lot. It told him that the suspect would go to great lengths to remove Colin from the picture, and that they were being watched.

~

Draco laughed and turned off his computer. He was going to have a lot of fun with the Scotsman. Happy to have a worthy adversary for once, two if he counted the lovely Cassidy. He headed downstairs to help Mary take care of Harold.

"My dear man." Draco patted the bound man on the shoulder. "I hope you understand that we can't allow you to roam the streets after finding out what our little group is about. Perhaps...God will help you." He laughed, remembering the man's parting words.

Harold squealed under his gag and cast a wide-eyed glance at poor Mary. The woman had made an attempt to appear more attractive, but the mustard-yellow blouse she wore did nothing for her complexion. Some people were doomed to be ugly. People like Draco. He ran a finger over the thick scar on his face. He'd been handsome once. Women had thrown themselves at him. No more. Now, people like him would rule the world; driven and powerful with the need for revenge.

He picked up a filet knife from the coffee table and stepped onto the plastic around Harold's chair. "I'm going to teach you patience, Mary. Now, you don't need to take your time with your victims. A quick, clean death is good enough, but after your overkill...well, you need to learn to take your time, just a little." He ran the thin blade down Harold's arm. Tiny drops of blood beaded in the cut.

"Have you ever fileted a fish, Mary? No? Well, you insert the knife like so..."

Harold screamed under his gag as Draco shaved off a layer of skin.

Draco handed the knife to Mary. "Practice, dear. I'll watch from the sofa. Don't make a mess. The less mess, the less we have to clean up."

Like an indulgent father, he watched his prodigy work.

6

Cassidy filled her mug with coffee and took a seat in the conference room. The FBI wanted everyone involved in the recent murders to watch the latest snuff film together. It wasn't exactly the way she preferred to start her morning.

Agent Ingram directed everyone's attention to the big screen at one end of the room, then pushed play on his computer. The other two FBI agents stood on each side of the screen like bookends.

Cassidy set her mug down and picked up her pen to jot notes. A person in black approached the woman tied to a tree and paused as if to say something, a hand holding an axe raised in preparation. The victim's mouth opened in a silent scream as the axe fell.

"That killer is a woman," Cassidy said. "She's still dressed in black as the first killer, but definitely a woman. Look at the hands and the way she carries herself."

"Good observation, Detective." Agent Ingram gave a grim smile. "We believe we are dealing with more than one perpetrator. The motive is still unclear."

"The words at both crime scenes gives us the motive," Colin said, taking a seat next to Cassidy. "The pretty must die. The answer we need to find is why? What do these people have against goodlooking people?"

"Revenge of some sort?" Cassidy took a sip of her coffee and grimaced. Their receptionist must make the worst coffee ever. "Perhaps they were wronged in some way?"

"Why are they targeting you, Detective Monroe?" Agent Ingram crossed his muscled arms. "Yes, we know your house was bugged and that Detective MacKenzie has updated your security system."

Cassidy cut a sideways glance at Colin. Traitor. "I believe these murders are somehow connected to my mother's murder ten years ago. The same words were found next to her body."

Ingram nodded. "I want MacKenzie with you at all times. He'll be moving into your home after this meeting."

"Sir!" No way. Cassidy valued her privacy and independence. She liked things done a certain way. Another person would disrupt all that.

"No arguments. Meeting adjourned."

"Shut up." Cassidy glared at Colin, who grinned like an idiot, and gathered her things. "We have work to do."

"What's on the agenda?"

"Have you checked the newspaper today?"

"Yes, and nothing."

"Why do you think that is?" She moved from the conference room and down the hall to the office she shared with Colin.

"The first killer places the ads for his own reasons. The second killer chose her victim." He perched on the corner of her desk, moving when Cassidy stared at the desk, then him.

"Got another body," Ingram called on his way past the office. "Out near Highway 64."

Colin grabbed the jeep keys from Cassidy's desk and dashed out before she could take them back. She was supposed to live with him? Impossible.

They followed the FBI agents to a culvert that ran under the highway. The air filled with the slamming of car doors as everyone emerged and converged on the crime scene.

Cassidy slid down the embankment and stared at the body of a man skinned like a fish. "This is different." She squatted next to the body. "Every murder is different. The amount of time it took to do this. It can't be the same killer as the one who used the ax." Unless the second killer was evolving, and very quickly.

No one could call the man goodlooking, either. A bulbous nose and overweight, he reminded her a bit of the cartoon character Mr. Toad.

"Not connected?" Agent Ingram stood next to her.

"It doesn't make sense. Until this week, Clear Springs had a low crime rate. Murders were unheard of." She stood. "Now, we have three in as many days." She scanned the treeline, the hairs on the back of her neck standing at attention. She withdrew her weapon and darted into the trees.

"After her, MacKenzie," Ingram called out. "You are her shadow until these killers are caught."

The crashing of the brush told Cassidy that Colin followed without her having to look back. She'd thought she'd spotted a flash of blue. The snap of a twig ahead of her spurred her on.

Another flash of blue.

She ran faster, catching sight of the back of a man's head. "Stop! Police!"

The man didn't pause, instead, firing a wild shot over his shoulder.

Cassidy dropped to the forest floor and aimed. Her shot missed. By the time Colin pulled her to her feet, the man was gone. "After him." She raced away.

The man seemed to have disappeared into thin air. The only evidence he had been there were a few broken branches and her sighting. She groaned.

"He's always at the scene," she said. "I know that now."

"Unfortunately, all we need is another body in order to prove that fact." Colin turned to head back to the crime scene. "We'll catch him. We can set a trap."

"He's been free for ten years." She glared up at him. "What makes you think we'll succeed this time?"

He grinned. "Because ten years ago, you weren't out to get him."

She snorted and ducked her head to hide her smile. The man had a way with words.

"That was the dumbest thing I've ever seen." Ingram confronted her the moment she stepped from the trees. "What part of don't go anywhere alone do you not understand?"

"I saw an opportunity and took it." She put the safety on her gun and re-holstered it. "That's what we do."

"Not anymore. You're valuable to this case. We need you to draw this guy out of the woodwork."

"I'm not going to be bait, Agent." She shook her head and climbed back to the road to retrieve her case so she could photograph the scene. She'd had the same thought herself, and had decided against it. She'd rather the perp came to her.

Bait. Ha! She'd find this freak and take him down. That was a promise she would do everything in her power to fulfill.

~

Colin had acted immediately when Cassidy ran into the trees. He hadn't needed Ingram's order. He'd been given the tasks of keeping her safe and catching a killer. Both things which he took very seriously. He might joke and flirt, but bringing this perp to justice before more lives were lost, was top priority.

Since the accidental shooting of an innocent bystander two years ago, Colin took every aspect of his job seriously. Too much, sometimes. In fact, he lost sleep over it more times than not.

He strolled slowly around the crime scene. “Cassidy. Here’s a footprint. Looks like a woman’s size nine.”

“You know that by looking?”

“Experience.” He squatted next to the print. “The same woman as beside Samantha Meyers, maybe?”

“We didn’t find any prints there.” She snapped a photograph. “This man is not pretty by any means.”

He shrugged. “I still say it’s the same perp. Why else would someone watch here, same as the second murder? This man got in the way somehow.”

Cassidy stood. “Perhaps. I don’t want to jump to any conclusions.”

“Are you acting this way because I’ll be living with you?” He couldn’t think of another reason for the cold shoulder or short answers.

She whirled. “I’m not helpless. I don’t need a bodyguard or a live in nanny. But, no, I’m not acting in any particular way because of that.”

“Hogswallow.”

“Excuse me?” Her eyes narrowed.

“That’s a load of bull. You’re mad and acting like a child because you can’t have things your way for a while.” He smirked and headed for the car.

“Trouble in paradise?” Ingram grinned.

“It’s your fault. You should be the one living with Miss Prickles.” Colin slid into the driver’s seat.

While he waited, he ran through his mind what they knew as facts. Three different murders, three different methods. Two were lured with modeling advertisements. The third did not fit the same MO as the girls. The authorities were dealing with a man and a woman perp. What they didn't know was…were the man and woman working together? Colin felt they were. The first two were killed because of their looks, the third…He rubbed his chin. Had the man known something he shouldn't or simply been in the wrong place at the wrong time? If the later, then why the meticulous skinning? That took time. They could have been caught. They would have needed a place no one would discover them or hear the man's screams.

Cassidy sat in the passenger seat and slammed her door. "I can see the steam coming from your ears. What are you thinking?"

He told her his thoughts. "I know you don't like to hear this, but I think Agent Ingram is right. We need you to draw this perp out."

"He'll never fall for it. He knows who I am. If I show up looking like Barbie, he won't make a move. What I look like won't change his plans."

"I'm sure Ingram is going to want to try."

"Where to now? We have no leads, no suspects, no one to question." Cassidy pounded the dashboard. "The man's a ghost, a vapor that dissipates in the trees."

"He's flesh and blood." Colin started the engine and pulled onto the highway. "Let's take a look at your mother's caseboard again. There has to be something we're missing."

"I've gone over that board a thousand times."

"Maybe so, but I'm new eyes, and this is a new case."

They drove in silence to her house. Colin exited the car first, then scanned the area while Cassidy unlocked the front door and disabled the alarm.

Once inside, he set the alarm and followed her to the basement.

"Someone's been in here," she said. "How did they get past the alarm?"

That was something Colin intended to find out. He pressed the buttons on his phone to the security agency.

~

How Draco loved her spirit! He stared at the photo in his hand. So like her mother in that regard.

He replaced the photo in his shirt pocket, then rolled the man into the shallow ditch. No amount of security could keep him from going where he wanted. A little painful pressure and the man had squealed like the pig he was and revealed the alarm code.

Why must dear Cassie think that something as simple as an alarm would keep him out? Perhaps, it was time to send her another letter. Something to relieve the fear she must feel. Surely, she knew he thought of her every single day of her life?

If only he hadn't rested for ten years, planning to fulfill his calling. Still, now was not the time to reveal himself. He'd been so careful, so meticulous.

He kicked rocks over the body. The cops would start to put the pieces together soon. He needed to make sure Mary took the rap before that happened. Oh, dear, Mary, already chomping at the bit to make her next kill.

The woman's overzealous nature was a hindrance. One Draco would have to curb in time.

He turned on the device in his ear and listened to the Scotsman as he combed Cassidy's house for recording devices. A waste of time. Draco was a dragon. Powerful and invincible. No mere mortal could foil his plans. But, let the little man try. It provided entertainment.

Draco returned to his Mercedes and headed to his luxury apartment in a nearby town. It wouldn't do to live too close to his darling. After his disfigurement so many years ago, he'd worked hard to amass a fortune in computer software. Now, while he sought his revenge against those who looked down on the less attractive, he had no worries about money. He had all the time in the world.

He laughed and cranked up his radio. Beethoven's Fifth shot from the disc player. Draco drummed his fingers along with the beat and sped home. Things were about to get exciting!

Pressing a button on his steering wheel, he sent a text to his followers.

Delete after reading. Consequences are tough. Meeting in usual place at nine a.m.

Things were gonna get shaken up for sure! He turned the volume on his radio higher and increased his speed. It was a good day to be a dragon.

7

Cassidy stared at the spot on the case board where her mother's picture had been. Scrawled in red sharpie was the word Dragon. Stories said dragons could be killed. She wanted to be the dragon slayer. She *would* bring this beast down. "I'm checking the rest of the house."

"There's no answer at the security agency." Colin slipped his phone in his pocket. "I'm coming with you, then we're paying a visit to my friend."

She nodded and headed upstairs, weapon in hand. Not that she expected to find anyone. This particular dragon came and went like a whisper.

Her bedroom closet was closed, same as her drawers. She opened them anyway and went through the items one-by-one. "I'm missing a pair of underwear."

"Laundry?" Colin peered into the drawer.

She slammed it shut. "I just did the laundry." She definitely didn't want him ogling her panties. "I don't know when they went missing, only that they are. Sick pervert." Some criminals took souvenirs, she just hadn't expected something of hers to be valuable enough to anyone. Why was this unsub fixated on her?

If she were to suffer the same fate as her mother, why hadn't he come forward and made a move? Why flit in and out of her house or spy on her at crime scenes? What had the man had against Cassidy's mother?

She moved into the bathroom. Everything looked to be in place.

"I'm taking the room right next to yours," Colin said. "Anyone after you, has to pass my room first."

"Fine." She still didn't like it, but saw the need for protection with every passing minute. "Let's go see why your friend's security measures didn't work." Although locking the door seemed a waste of time, she did it on their way out anyway. The Dragon had proven he would go where he wanted. "The next stop is the pound. I'm adopting the biggest, meanest dog they have. That's the best security."

Colin shrugged. "I'm the best security, but I like dogs. Instead of the pound, I know a guy who sells German Shepherds. They're well trained to listen to commands and not to take food from anyone other than their owner. That way, they can't be poisoned."

"How far?"

"About an hour."

They made the drive to Colin's security acquaintance in silence and pulled up in front of a modest bungalow. Cassidy cut the engine. "He works out of his home?"

"Yep. Wait until you see what's in his garage." Colin bounded from the jeep and hurried to the front door. He knocked, then peered through the front window before trying the doorknob. The door swung open. He exchanged a grim look with Cassidy, then pulled his gun.

"Stay behind me," he said.

Cassidy pulled her own weapon and walked so close to him she could smell his aftershave. Tension radiated off Colin's back, rippling his muscles.

They made their way through the three bedroom house, eventually ending up in a garage filled floor to ceiling with computer monitors and surveillance equipment. This was no small time security company.

Colin moved to the monitors and typed something on one of the computers. Video of Cassidy's house popped up. A few more buttons and the video showed a man in black punching in the security code on the keypad inside her front door. Seconds later, he headed down the basement steps, took a few minutes to study the case board, then snatched the photo and strolled out of the house as if he had all the time in the world.

"This killer has nerves of steel." Colin pounded the desktop. "Let's go get that dog."

"What about your friend?"

"I have no idea where to look for him. Either he's out on an innocent errand or he's dead. We won't know until he answers my phone call or we find his body." He stormed out of the house.

Cassidy took one more look at the video feed of her house, then followed. The killer was always one step ahead of them. They needed a huge break in the case.

"I'm sorry about your friend," she said, sliding into the passenger seat and letting Colin drive.

"We don't know that anything bad has happened." A muscle ticked in his jaw.

Cassidy knew, deep in her gut, that the man was dead. The Dragon didn't leave witnesses. He'd found out about the security, killed Colin's friend, then strolled into her house as if he were an honored guest.

Their next stop took them to a ranch in the mountains. Colin drove the jeep down a dirt road and stopped in front of an A-frame log cabin. While dogs milled around the yard, not one barked as Cassidy and Colin exited the jeep.

A man stepped onto the porch. "Hey, Scot! This the lady that needs a protector?"

Cassidy pasted on a smile. "A female dog, if possible." The last thing she needed was a dog lifting its leg on everything in sight.

"I've got the perfect girl for you." He motioned for them to follow. "Her name is Rosie. She won't bark unless you tell her to guard, then she'll alert you the moment someone steps foot on your property. If you want her to attack, say Angriff, that's German for attack, and motion toward the person you want a hurting put on. Say watch 'em for her to watch. If you want any other command words, teach her. She's a smart girl, two years old, and will catch on quick."

He unlocked a gate leading into a large dog run. “Take care of her and she’ll take care of you. Rosie!” A beautiful dog with straight ears, a regal head, and a prominent black saddle against a dark tan body trotted toward them.

Cassidy held out her hand, already in love with her new best friend. “Hello, Rosie. How will she know I’m hers?”

“The moment I clip her leash on her collar and hand it to you, she’ll know. She’ll be loyal to death, ma’am.” He clipped a bright red leash to a matching collar and handed it to Cassidy.

The moment the dog stared up at her with trusting, wise eyes, Cassidy knew she’d do everything in her power to keep Rosie safe. “Thank you, girl. We’ll make a good team.”

~

Colin couldn’t help feeling a twinge of jealousy at Cassidy’s words. He wanted her to think of him as a good partner. What held her back? While she remained professional at all times, he often wondered why her hesitancy in opening up to him. They’d be together twenty-four seven until the silly dragon was caught.

His cell phone rang the same time Cassidy’s did. He pulled it from his pocket and read the text. “Another body.” He’d bet his teeth it was Seth Jargon, his security friend.

“That dog will track, too,” the trainer said. “Not much my furry children can’t do. They’re as docile as lambs until you want them to work.”

"Great. Come on, girl. We have a job to do." Cassidy opened the back door of the jeep for the dog, then slid back into the passenger seat.

Colin informed Agent Ingram they were an hour out, then took his place in the driver's seat. "Let's see what our new partner can do."

Driving above the speed limit, they reached the location where the FBI agents waited in forty minutes. Colin headed into a ditch, leaving Cassidy to bring the dog.

"A new friend?" Ingram motioned his head toward Rosie.

"I thought it a good idea." Colin peeled back the blanket covering the body and stared into the lifeless face of his friend. "This is Seth Jargon. He owns Secret Eyes Security. I hired him to install an alarm system in Detective Monroe's house. A security system that the perpetrator got around, strolled in, and stole a photograph of Monroe's mother." He straightened. "That's been our day."

"The victim died from what looks like a single gunshot to the heart. The ME can tell us more, but if it's the same perp, he's all over the place in his MO."

"The Dragon." Cassidy led the dog around the perimeter of the body. "He calls himself The Dragon."

Rosie's ears perked up, and she froze, staring into the trees.

"Let's go, Colin." Cassidy unhooked the leash and motioned for the dog to go. Like a rocket, Rosie shot into the trees, Cassidy following at a run.

Colin dashed after them. Just like the last time, they crashed through the brush to no avail. If anyone had been there, they disappeared, which became evident the moment Rosie stopped and looked up at Cassidy with a whine.

She glanced over her shoulder at Cassidy who patted her on the head. “Good girl.” She reattached the leash to the collar, then turned to Colin. “I’m getting very frustrated with all this.” She stomped past him.

“We’ll get a team out here to scour the woods. Maybe they’ll find something to help us. The man is bound to have left something behind.” Not that it would do much good to find DNA on someone not in the system. But, it would tell them they were chasing the same person responsible for the other deaths.

“I’m going to have the locks changed on my house and change the security code. If he doesn’t have anyone to kill in order to get the needed information, it might make it harder for him to get inside.”

“Have Rosie at your side at all times. Between me and the dog, you’ll be safe.”

She sighed. “I’m not worried about me, Colin. I want this man caught so the murders stop.”

She might not be worried about herself, but Colin was losing sleep at night. He couldn’t lose a partner. Between worrying about Cassidy and the nightmares that plagued him, it was a wonder he could think straight.

They rejoined the FBI agents as the body was being loaded into an ambulance. He hadn’t known

Seth well, not being in the states more than a year, but his heart lurched to see someone he'd shared beers and laughs with zipped into a black bag and stowed away. He didn't want that to happen to Cassidy. He steeled his heart against caring too much and marched to the jeep.

~

Draco looked over his group of nine. He preferred an odd number. Every form of art looked better in odd numbers. But, Harold had betrayed them. Soon, Mary would have to go, once she'd served her purpose. Then, he'd need to recruit another.

"When will I have my turn?" Ben, a man whose face was pitted with acne scars, scowled.

"Patience. Mary has almost completed her tasks, right Mary?"

She nodded. "One more. I'm ready. I've proven myself with Harold."

Draco sighed. "We do not say the names out loud of those who have left us."

Silence descended over the room as the implications of Mary's slip of the tongue registered on the attendees. No matter. They needed to know the price of disobedience.

"It is often difficult to mete out punishment," Draco said, "even when the person needs it. In order to help you all take the next step, I've designed some tasks for you to fulfill. Jobs that will help you face your adversary and inact your revenge without showing that you are a novice. In the jar on the table are slips of paper. Each of you are to draw one. On it, you will find your assigned task. Don't disappoint me, people." He fixed a stern gaze on them. "Show me you can do these things. Show me you can stay one step ahead of the police. Only this will prove that you are worthy to be my follower."

Chairs scraped along the floor of Draco's rented house. Not the place he called home, but rather his place of business. His followers formed a line and each took a slip of paper that would cause chaos in the town of Clear Springs.

A grin spread across his face. If his beloved Cassidy could continue with her bravery despite the coming disasters, she would prove her worth.

8

Cassidy sat on the basement floor, boxes piled around her. Rosie lay staring at her with big dark eyes.

She hadn't slept a wink. Colin might have been in the next room but Cassidy couldn't have been more aware of him if he'd snored in the same bed. What was wrong with her? She'd sworn off men for the sake of her career. Why would one handsome Scotsman with a sexy brogue and deep blue eyes rock her plans?

"Coffee?" As if her thoughts had called him, the object of her lack of sleep handed her a steaming mug. "What are you doing?"

"Thanks." She took the drink. "Going back through my mother's files. I must have missed something. With the new evidence, I thought it worth the time."

Colin sat cross-legged across from her and pulled a box to him. "It's as good a plan as any."

Concentration was in short supply. Cassidy sneaked a peek at the man across from her. His dark hair was ruffled from sleep, his tee shirt faded, and baggy plaid lounge pants covered his long legs. She'd never seen anyone sexier. She sighed and dug further into the box.

"I haven't looked through everything," she admitted. "Some of these boxes are my mother's personal effects. It was too painful...until now." It was still painful, but needed to be done in the light of the current situation.

"I can do this if its too hard." Colin gave her a lopsided grin. "I had to go through my parents' things a few years back. Most difficult thing I ever did."

"I'm sorry about your parents. How did they die?"

"House fire." He sighed. "It was arson. They arrested a disgruntled neighbor a few days later. The man was angry over boundary lines."

"That's rough." They shared the fact both of their families were murdered. In an uncharacteristic gesture, Cassidy reached over and placed her hand on his. "The pain never goes away, does it?"

"Never." He handed her a leather book. "This looks like a journal. You should be the one to read it."

Her hand shook as she took the journal and flipped it open. "It's my mother's." She scooted against the wall and started to read while Colin continued looking through the boxes. An hour later, she froze. This couldn't be right.

She read the words again. "I'm a product of rape." She flipped through the pages again. "No name of her attacker, though." The book fell into her lap. "Why didn't she ever tell me?"

"What?" Colin stopped what he was doing.

"My mother wrote about the experience. She chose to keep me despite the violent act. Fought and injured the man and got away. That's why she became a cop, so she could help victims." Her eyes burned as her heart sank to her knees. "When I asked about my father, she always put me off, saying she'd tell me about him someday."

Who was Cassidy's father? Had they ever caught him? That was one mystery she might never know. Still, her gut told her she knew the man, had seen him before. Would she recognize physical traits they shared?

She shook off her thoughts and set the journal aside. They had multiple murders to solve. She could explore her genealogy at another time.

"Here's something." Colin handed her a yellowed newspaper page. "Your mother answered an advertisement. The same as our first two victims."

Cassidy snatched the paper. "But our victims weren't sexually assaulted."

"Maybe he's too old." Colin gave a wry grin. "Can't...you know."

"Don't be crude." She set the paper next to the journal. "My mother was almost twenty when she had me. Right around the same age as our victims. He's evolved. More in control of his actions."

"I agree. It was a poor joke." He closed the box and reached for another one. "We need to check the police records at the time your mother was attacked, then later when she was murdered. See what the officers thought about the situation."

"I've read everything I could find on her murder, but didn't know about the rape. We'll go when we've finished these boxes." They might find something else to help them in their search.

They didn't. By the time they finished going through the boxes they'd uncovered nothing more of interest other than the journal and the newspaper. "I'm hitting the shower," Cassidy said, "then I'll be ready to dig through the police files."

"I'm making more coffee and omelets. You have to be starving." He unfolded his lean frame and took her hand, pulling her to her feet.

Handsome and could cook? "I am hungry." She bounded up the steps, taking the book and paper with her and hurried to the bathroom.

She couldn't help but glance in every crevice and corner for hidden cameras. No way did she want The Dragon, she smirked at his name, to see her in the shower. She turned the water to hot and disrobed, draping the shorts and tee shirt she'd slept in over the toilet.

Adjusting the faucet to a comfortable temperature, she stepped into the shower, wrapped her arms around her middle, and cried. No wonder her mother hadn't wanted to talk about Cassidy's father. How horrifying the experience must have been. A young woman right out of high school, her future promising, attacked and left pregnant by a monster.

She raised her face to the spray and let the water wash away her tears. She'd managed to hold it together with Colin, but now, alone, she let the grief swamp her. When her tears were spent, she washed her hair and body and toweled dry.

She stepped out of the room to the aroma of frying bacon. So far, having Colin around hadn't been a hardship other than her heightened awareness of him. She took a deep breath and squared her shoulders. She couldn't let her emotions run rampant around him. Caring for another only opened one's heart to ache.

~

The vulnerability on his partner's face when she'd read the journal had ripped at his heart. He'd wanted to comfort her, but knowing that wouldn't go over well, had told a bad joke instead. What was wrong with him? He wasn't usually an insensitive person.

He flipped the omelet onto a plate and set it in the oven to keep warm while he cooked the second one. When Cassidy perched on a stool at the breakfast bar, he removed the first omelet and slid it to her. "Feel better?"

"A little."

"Must have been a shock." He wanted to comfort her the same way he did the relatives of murdered victims. But, Cassidy was different. No simple pat on the hand would suffice. Not when he wanted to pull her into his arms and cradle her against his chest. With her standoffish attitude, that wasn't a good idea.

She fed a bite of egg to the dog. Having the biggest German Shepherd he'd ever laid eyes on, one that was trained to protect, eased his mind somewhat. He wouldn't need to keep his eyes on his partner every second if Rosie was around.

His omelet finished, he sat on a stool next to Cassidy and dug into his breakfast. “Scanning old newspapers will be time consuming, but all we need is a little something to help us along.”

“I think we need to question the friends.” Cassidy left a few bites on her plate and set it on the floor for Rosie to lick clean. “I know we did preliminary questions, and that they all said they hadn’t seen the victims the night they died, but I want to dig deeper.”

“I don’t think they know the killer. The victims were both visiting family here.”

“I know, but I’m at a dead end here, Colin.” Her face was lined with stress.

“I’m starting to agree with Ingram.” He eyed the loose pants and shirt she had on. “I think you need to start dressing like one of the pretty people and lure this freak out of hiding.”

She sighed. “Such a bother. I worked hard to get where I’m at in my career. Looking like a fashion plate won’t help me be taken seriously.”

“It’s all about the attitude.” He grinned. “If you act kick ass, people will think you are. You can do that in stilettos as well as work boots.”

“Stilettos are out of the question. I’ll break my neck.” She slid from the stool. “I’ll go see what I have in my closet. There may be a shopping trip in my future.”

He laughed. “You make that sound like a death sentence.”

“It is.” She motioned for Rosie to follow, and left the kitchen.

The doorbell rang. Colin waited for Cassidy to give the order for Rosie to guard. When it didn't come, he peered out the peephole in the door. Most killers didn't ring the doorbell.

Agent Ingram stood on the porch, the other two agents waiting by the car. This did not look good.

Colin opened the door. "Sir?"

"Mail for Monroe." He handed Colin a large Manilla envelope. "We've scanned it for anything hazardous. Seems clean, but we thought she should open it right away."

"She's upstairs getting dressed. Come on in." Colin turned and almost stumbled over Rosie. Good girl. Silent as a wraith and as vigilant as the best cop. Her eyes never left Ingram.

"There's coffee in the kitchen," Colin said. "Will Smith and Weston be coming in?" He couldn't say their names without grinning.

"No. They're on guard duty, but I'd love a cup."

Soon, they sat at the breakfast bar, sipping coffee, waiting for Cassidy to come downstairs. Colin told Ingram their plans on looking through old newspaper articles, but left out the full reason why. He also explained about wanting to question friends and family deeper.

"This case is a tough one," Ingram said. "Bodies are piling up, no evidence is left behind, we're dealing with more than one perp, and we're getting nowhere."

"We can't give up." Cassidy stepped into the room. Her makeup had been artfully applied, her hair straightened down her back in an curtain of fire. A navy blue suit fit her as if tailored for her. A sea green blouse complimented her eyes.

Colin's gaze flicked to her feet. The same black work boots. Still, the woman was stunning.

Ingram smiled. "You clean up nice, Monroe."

"This had better work." She poured coffee into a travel thermos. "It takes three times as long to get ready when I have to go to this kind of trouble."

"At least the view is better." Ingram clapped her on the shoulder. "Let's go to work."

~

Draco stood in the shadows between two buildings across the street from the bank and watched as two of his followers tossed a pipe bomb through the open door of a vacant building. No one would be injured...this time, but it would bring his darling Cassidy running to the scene.

The two doing his bidding jumped into a waiting car and sped away as people flocked onto the sidewalk to see what the commotion was about. Fifteen minutes later, the FBI crows in the black suits and black SUV pulled up, followed by Cassidy and her partner in the jeep.

Draco smiled as his darling exited the vehicle, looking like one of the FBI agents. Only, her beauty shown as radiate as the fire spewing from the bombed building's shattered windows. Yes, he had a personal grievance against beautiful people, but despite her professional demeanor, Cassidy Monroe was more beautiful on the inside than out. He'd seen her care for the citizens of Clear Springs. Watched as she put in more than one hundred percent effort in catching criminals. Beautiful, yes, but smart, and...his.

With one last adoring glance at her, he turned and headed down the alley toward his car. The pipe bomb was only the beginning. He needed to supervise the next follower's orders. He rubbed his hands together. It was going to be wonderful!

"Hey, mister! You can't park there." A man in a white apron exited the back door of the bakery. "Employees only. Can't you read?"

Keeping his face averted, Draco tossed the man a flippant wave and sped from the alley. Now, he'd have to drive his second favorite car. The baker was bound to have gotten the make and model of the car. Not the license plate, though. He grinned. That he kept too dirty to read.

9

"Stay." Cassidy commanded Rosie to remain in the car and shut the door, leaving the window open against the warm morning, then turned to survey the hectic scene.

Flames billowed from the storefront and ate at the roof. Glass littered the sidewalk like confetti. "Was anyone injured or killed?"

One of the first responders, an EMT she had yet to meet, answered, "No. Just an explosion."

"Any witnesses?"

"That baker over there came running over a minute ago. He's waiting to talk to someone."

She nodded and headed for the man in a white apron. "Sir, I'm Detective Monroe. Do you have information for us?"

He glanced toward the alley. "I'm not sure it's related, but right after the explosion, I saw a man in a dark Mercedes speeding out of the alley. I called to him to stop, but he kept going. Customers are not allowed in the alley."

"License plate?"

"Too dirty to see." The man frowned. "That was the strange part. The rest of the car, and the man, were immaculate."

"Rosie!" Cassidy motioned for the dog and Colin to join her. "Thank you, sir. You've been very helpful."

Rosie bounded from the car window and sprinted to Cassidy's side a second before Colin joined her. The three of them headed into the alley as Cassidy explained what the witness saw.

The alley was empty of all but a few cars, none of them a Mercedes. Not that Cassidy expected to see the perpetrator still hanging around. While Colin studied the tire tracks, she began the arduous task of knocking on business doors.

She hit pay dirt on door number three. An elderly lady who smelled of chocolate answered.

"I saw a rusty pickup truck pull away from across the street seconds before the explosion," she explained. "It had two men inside. I think they were men."

"Why didn't you report this when the authorities showed up?" Cassidy's pencil poised over her notepad.

"I didn't know if there would be more explosions. I'm a simple candy store owner, not a vigilante. Finding these people is your job."

"Yes, ma'am, and we're doing our best but we can always use the help of the community."

"That's not what my tax dollars pay for." She slammed the door.

Cassidy shook her head. Two vehicles, one luxury, one not, were seen fleeing the scene. Which one, or both, were involved?

She scanned up and down the alley. "Do you think it's The Dragon?" How she hated that name.

"No clue. He didn't leave us much to go on, if it is." Colin straightened and snapped a picture of the tire tracks. "Let's head back to the station. I still need to look through the morning's paper, and you can get started on the old issues."

She nodded and glanced in the direction the Mercedes had gone. A sheet of paper danced on a slight breeze. Following her instinct, she darted for it, chasing the paper until it stopped against a cement wall. She lifted it by the corner. Printed on it were the words:

Detective Monroe:

Are you enjoying our little game? Can you prove yourself worthy to be my assailant? We have more in common than you know.

Draco

"It *was* him." She said, hurrying back to Colin and handing him the note. "He's playing a silly game."

Colin's mouth twisted in thought. "No one died, which leaves me to believe he didn't want them to. When he kills, it's personal."

"Personal to his accomplices, too." Cassidy sighed. How could she keep up with the man without clues? A single sheet of paper and a set of tire tracks wouldn't reveal his identity. "I can look for someone in the system named Draco, but I'm sure it's an alias." They didn't even have enough for Rosie to track. She bit back a curse. Her mother had once told her that if you had to curse to be interesting, then you weren't interesting to begin with. Still, times that like this made it difficult to keep a civil tongue.

Most people in law enforcement cursed with regularity. Cassidy was determined to be different. Not only in the way she handled herself, but in how she did her job. She glanced heavenward. *I could use some help right about now*. From her mother, from God, she wasn't picky.

After letting Agent Ingram know about the note and statements from the witnesses, Cassidy opened the door to the jeep to let Rosie in, then climbed in herself. The note proved The Dragon was responsible. Thus, the FBI could supervise casing the scene, freeing her and Colin to head back to the station.

Once there, she made a pot of coffee, filled two mugs, and joined her partner in front of the case board they worked on with the FBI. After handing Colin his coffee, she tacked up the note and two cards with the descriptions of the vehicles. Perching on her desk, she sipped her coffee and studied the board. Nothing but murders and games.

She sighed and sat at her desk, opening her laptop and logging into the site that gave her access to old newspapers. She typed in her mother's name and started searching.

She stopped on the article about her mother's rape. Not a rape by a stranger, but one at a college fraternity party. Her mother said she hadn't known the man, but had fought back until several other college young men heard the ruckus. By that time, Mom was covered in blood…not hers.

Cassidy needed to find the young men who found her. No names, but someone at the college had to know something. She picked up the phone and called Arkansas State. Fifteen minutes later, she had the name of a teacher who had been there at the time of the rape who agreed to speak with her.

"Let's go to college." She grabbed her purse and weapon, clipped the leash on Rosie's collar, and headed out the door.

"I really hate when you do that," Colin said, jogging to catch up.

"Do what?" She cut him a sideways glance.

"Take off like I'm going to follow like an obedient puppy."

"Aren't you going to follow?"

"That isn't the point." He scowled, his brows lowering over his amazing eyes. "It's rude."

"Sorry. I'll try to do better, but we have an appointment." She explained what she found. "Maybe this teacher saw or heard something that will take us a step further in this investigation."

~

They parked in front of the administration building, then asked the receptionist inside where to find the cafeteria. She glanced at Cassidy's badge before pointing them in the right direction. She frowned at Rosie, but didn't say anything, then turned back to her work.

The cafeteria was virtually empty that time of day. Cassidy headed for a man who looked to be nearing his retirement years. "Mr. Laraby?"

"Yes. I presume you're Detective Monroe." He waved them to the two empty chairs at his table. "Beautiful dog. A service animal?"

"In a sense." Cassidy took her seat. "You knew Maureen Monroe?"

"She was one of my students. A very bright girl. I was saddened to hear of her murder." He straightened in his chair and crossed his arms. "You believe her rapist killed her?"

Cassidy nodded. "What can you tell us about the night she was attacked?"

He sighed. "It was a frat party. Your mother came with a friend. The other gal ditched her and ran off with her boyfriend. Not sure how Maureen occupied herself. All I know is that three young men came running, one of them carrying her. She was covered in blood. We discovered it wasn't hers. When the cops arrived, she told them what happened and that she cut her attacker." He gave a wry smile. "She was one tough girl."

"We know all this. I was hoping you could tell us something new. Who were the boys?"

"Only one is alive right now. One died in a car crash, the other in Desert Storm. Bruce Main lives a few blocks from here." He scribbled an address on Cassidy's notepad. "I doubt he can tell you much more. I don't think anyone got a good look at the attacker."

"Was he as student here?"

"Very possible. It wasn't a secret party, but you did have to be enrolled here to attend. Still, it wouldn't have been impossible for someone to sneak in." He slid a thick book across the table. "A yearbook I 'borrowed' from the library. Good luck."

Cassidy shook his hand, thanked him, and glanced at Colin. "Ready to make one more stop?"

"No stone unturned." He grinned.

~

Colin stared at the small white house. A tricycle sat on a well-manicured lawn. If the man was married with children, he might not be happy to dredge up something horrible from his past. Still, Cassidy deserved to know as much as possible. He shoved open the car door.

"Stay." Cassidy left Rosie on the front porch and rang the doorbell. The yearbook was tucked under her arm.

A man in a business suit opened the door. "I'm heading to work. Not buying whatever you're selling."

Colin flashed his badge. "We have a few questions. Are you Bruce Main?"

Surprise registered in the man's eyes. "Yes, but..." He closed the door and joined them on the porch. "I really have no idea why you're here."

"Mr. Main." Cassidy stepped forward. "You helped a woman who was attacked almost twenty-five years ago at a frat party. That woman was my mother. She was later murdered. I'd like to know what you can tell us about that night."

He rubbed the back of his neck. "Not much. Me and the boys heard her scream. When we got there, a dark-haired man was running into the bushes. I gave chase, but he got away. I'm afraid I'd been...intoxicated, and not too quick on my feet. I'm sorry."

"It wasn't your fault. Is there anything else you can tell me about her attacker? Did you recognize him? Would he be in this book?" She held out the yearbook.

Main glanced at Colin. "Man, this is bringing up some stuff I never wanted to think about again."

"I'm sorry, but it's important." Colin took the book from Cassidy and handed it to Main. "Please. Is there a place we can sit?"

"There's a table on the back porch. My wife has already left and the babysitter is inside. Will that suffice?"

"Perfect." Colin took Cassidy by the elbow and escorted her after the man. They sat quietly while he flipped through the thick book.

"I think it might be one of these two men." He tapped two pictures. "Loners, both of them, but they were at the party. I hate to accuse anyone when I didn't get a good look at his face, but the profiles...yeah, it could be one of them."

Colin glanced at the names. Daniel Haler and Vince Smith. Could one of them be the man they were looking for?

"Neither one of them returned to school after that night. With as much blood as Maureen had on her..." Main shuddered. "She hurt her attacker. If he would have come back to school, we would have known."

"Thank you." Cassidy stood and offered her hand. "You've been a big help."

He returned her shake and offered his hand to Colin. "I hope so. That's a night I'd rather forget. One more thing. There was a knife next to Maureen. We left it there. I'm not sure whether we ever told the cops. Like I said, we were drunk."

"Can you tell us how to get to where the attack took place?" Colin asked.

"Sure. It isn't far, but nature would have taken over. Or the police could have found the knife."

Cassidy shook her head. "Nothing in the files about a knife."

He gave them directions. "I really need to go. Good luck." He bounded down the stairs and to his car.

Cassidy grinned. "We're getting closer to slaying a dragon."

10

Cassidy knew the chances of finding the knife her mother used after that many years was slim. Still, she wanted to see the place she was conceived in violence. The place that changed everything she thought her life growing up had been. She glanced around the small patch of trees behind the college.

How dark it must have been. How frightened her mother must have been. Still, she'd fought for her life, not preventing her rape, but wounding her attacker. Fatally? Perhaps, but not likely. He was seen fleeing the scene. "I want to check emergency room and hospitals for knife wounds on that night," she said, turning to Colin. "If he'd been injured badly, he would have had to seek medical attention."

Colin glanced toward the college. "Not the first aid office here, most likely. We can make some calls back at the office."

She glanced around the area, trying to envision what had happened that night. Years of nature reclaiming her territory would have covered the knife in dirt and leaves. Without the proper equipment, if the knife was still there, they'd never find it.

"I'm ready to go." With a gentle tug on Rosie's leash, she headed back to the car.

They stopped for lunch at a fast food burger place and took their food to the conference room where the FBI agents waited for them. "About time," Ingram said.

"We were following a lead to nowhere." Cassidy opened her food sack and explained about their visit to the college.

Ingram frowned. "You think your biological father is this Dragon?"

She froze. She hadn't put the thought into words, but now that he said it, it made sense. "I don't know. Who else had a reason to kill my mother? The man she injured. If he's killing pretty people, maybe his knife wound was disfiguring. I'm going to check hospital records for that night."

"MacKenzie, what do you think?"

Colin exhaled sharply. "It's all connected somehow. Why else would The Dragon be focused on Cassidy?"

Ingram shrugged. "We'll go with it for now. Monroe, get a DNA sample on you. We'll have something to compare this Draco with if we ever get lucky. Maybe your DNA will match with that on the first victim's shoe."

She nodded and bit into her burger. "I really hope I'm wrong."

Colin opened the morning's paper while he ate. The agents left the room to process anything found at that morning's bombing and, hopefully, pursue Cassidy's hunch about Draco. Figures that she'd found out her biological father wasn't a military hero, but rather a sick, twisted killer.

Retrieving her laptop from her desk, she set it up on the conference table and began her search for knife victims almost twenty-five years ago. Eye strain set in almost immediately, and her focus wavered.

"Found another advertisement." Colin handed her the paper. "He's specifically asking for a red head. You, perhaps?"

She scanned the personal ad. "Red haired model wanted. Competitive pay. Come to 506 Oakwood Drive at eight p.m." It showed today's date. "It looks like I have an appointment tonight."

"Not without me and the agents." Colin took the paper back and tore out the ad.

"He won't be there." She shoved a french fry into her mouth. "It's a test to see if I'll show."

"Doesn't matter. You still aren't going alone."

"I wasn't planning on it." The Dragon was just crazy enough to kill her.

~

Oh, this was going to be good. Draco rubbed his hands together. He had no doubt sweet Cassidy would show. He'd hide behind a two way mirror and let one of his minions take the fall, if it came to that. A new man arrived to that morning's meeting, eager to prove his worth. If he could get in and out of a warehouse full of cops trying to hide, he'd be worthy to be a follower. If not, he'd die in a hail of bullets. Draco didn't care either way.

He placed a folding chair behind the wall size mirror and settled down to wait. That night's photographer sat quiet next to him, awaiting orders.

"Be vigilant, Mark. A precious woman will soon enter that cavernous room. She'll be beautiful…and armed. Do not harm her. Convince her that you are a photographer. If you can't, then find a way to flee. While you won't see the cops, they'll be there."

"I have a way out. A hidden door in the wall behind the backdrop. I won't fail you." The acne scarred, balding man met Draco's gaze. "I'll do this, then you help me rid the world of a witch."

"I promise." Draco smiled with pleasure at the thick scar running from the man's jaw to his collar bone. Cassidy would think this poor example of himself to be Draco. Imagine her surprise when she finally meets the real Dragon. "Get into place."

Mark nodded and stood, exiting through a side door as Cassidy stepped into the brightly lit room. "Welcome," he said, grinning. "My name is Mark, and I've a variety of gowns for you to wear."

~

Cassidy's gaze landed on the scar running along the man's neck. Was it possible Draco was actually showing himself? "I'd like a red one. Do you think it will clash with my hair?"

"No, I think it will be wonderful." His grin never faltered. "There's a changing screen there. We can start with red and move to other colors. You'll be a fabulous model. Those cheek bones..." he kissed his fingers.

Cassidy rolled her eyes and stepped behind the screen. What in the hell was going on? This man did not act like a cold blooded killer. Was it possible he really was a model scout? She chewed the inside of her cheek.

Outside, Colin and the others waited for her signal. What if she made a mistake and they converged on an innocent man? She needed to discover a way to determine whether this man was Draco or not?

"How did you get that scar?" she asked, stepping from behind the curtain. The red dress she'd chosen hugged her curves.

Mark turned his head and fiddled with a camera on a tripod. "Car accident."

"I'm sorry. It really isn't any of my business." She stood in front of a background depicting a misty forest. "I think my father has a similar scar." She forced a smile. "But, I've never actually met him. He got his in a fight, I heard."

Mark turned on a high powered fan. "Sounds like a bad ass."

She shrugged. "What would you like me to do?"

"Act sexy and stop talking."

Act sexy? One of the few things she had no idea how to do. She pursed her lips and lifted her hair from her neck while he snapped pictures. This was getting them nowhere.

"Have you been a photographer long? Do you have a portfolio?" She did her best to act empty-headed and flirtatious.

"Why are you talking to me?" Mark's friendly demeanor faded to be replaced with anger. "Don't I repulse you?"

She stopped moving. "No, should you?"

"The acne pits and scar doesn't turn you off?"

"No one is perfect, Mark. Some people's scars can't be seen."

"You seem to be perfect." He snapped another picture, then glanced at the mirror on the wall.

Cassidy smiled and approached the mirror, holding her fingertip to the glass. Ah ha. A two-way mirror. She turned. "Tell my father to come out and speak to me."

Mark's eyes widened.

The lights cut off.

"I need back up!" Cassidy called.

A door slammed somewhere in the dark.

She grappled for something to use as a weapon, her hand closing on the camera tripod. It would work in a pinch. She clutched it in one hand as she searched with the other for the changing screen. Her holster and gun hung on a hook just inside...there. She dropped the tripod and clutched the gun as the lights flickered back on.

Colin raced toward her, grabbed her arm, and tried to drag her from the building. "Let's get you safe."

"Wait." She grabbed her clothes. "It's the only suit I have."

They dashed outside as a dark-colored sedan sped away.

Cassidy groaned. "He wasn't Draco, but the man was there. That mirror is a two-way. What kind of game is he playing?"

Colin's gaze warmed as it raked over her. "You look very beautiful."

"Stop it. We're working."

~

Colin had listened to the recording coming clear through the wire Cassidy wore with interest. Realizing that Mark the photographer was not Draco The Dragon had been a brilliant move. "I don't know what game he's playing, but he's trying to get you to do something."

"He needs to face me and stop wasting our time." She leaned against the jeep as the FBI agents exited the building.

"I thought you looked good in a suit," Ingram said, grinning. "But, this...ooh, la la."

"Let's hurry this up so I can go home and change." Cassidy scowled. "Did you find anything?"

"A door behind the backdrop. That's how he got away. Good move on asking him about Draco. He also took the camera with him. Looks like dear old Dad wanted photos of his darling daughter."

"Let's go." Cassidy opened the door to the jeep. "I left Rosie at home and it feels weird without her."

Colin joined her. The agents would finish with the scene, as always. All Colin and Cassidy were good for was doing the grunt work. “Do you feel as if tonight was a waste of time?”

She shook her head. “We discovered that Draco does, indeed, have others working with or for him. I say that’s a huge discovery.”

They only needed to figure out what to do with the information. Colin started the ignition. “I think you were supposed to think Mark was Draco.”

“He’s not old enough or sure enough of himself. I figured out Draco was there by the way Mark’s eyes kept darting toward the mirror.” She propped her bare feet on the dashboard. “Draco wanted to see whether he could pull my strings. Fine. I’ll play along. Maybe by doing so, we can prevent more deaths.”

“I agree.” But, he didn’t like it. Not one bit. It was a dangerous game. One that could get them all killed.

He cut a sideways glance at the beautiful woman next to him. What were the thoughts and feelings running through her head? They had to be momentous. Finding out your father might be a serial killer had to do things to her head. He reached over and grasped her hand. “Are you okay?”

“I’m fine.” She stared out the window.

“It’s okay to not be fine.” He gave her hand a squeeze.

She pulled it away. “I’ve got a lot on my mind, Colin. Leave it alone. I’ll deal with it all once this maniac is behind bars.”

“Don’t push me away. I can help you through this.” He’d do whatever it took to keep her safe, help her sort out the information that had to have her reeling.

They stopped at a stop sign. He grabbed her hand again and pulled her close, staring into eyes illuminated by the street light.

"Don't," she whispered.

"Oh, but I'm going to. You need something else to think about." He pulled her a little closer.

"No."

"Yes." He moved his hand to the back of her head and placed his lips on hers. Gently, like a trainer would touch a skittish horse. He deepened the kiss, cupping her face.

She moaned and put her arms around his neck.

A horn honked behind them, pulling them out of the increasingly heated moment.

Cassidy jerked as if stung. "I can't do this. You can't distract me this way."

He chuckled. "I think I can." He pulled away from the stop sign, fully intending to continue distracting her from the myriad of problems running through her mind. She needed to focus on one thing—catching Draco. Their biological relationship needed to take a backseat right now.

If she sunk into a depressed state, which Colin suspected she was headed toward, they'd accomplish nothing.

11

"Let me get out of this dress," Cassidy said the moment they stepped into her house. "I'll meet you in the living room."

"I'll make popcorn." Colin grinned.

Still clutching her suit and boots, Cassidy hiked the dress to her knees and climbed the stairs to her room. Wadding the gown into a ball, she stuffed it into a paper bag and placed it in the corner before donning a pair of cotton shorts and a long tee shirt. The dress would go to the station in the morning for evidence. Not that they would find any prints other than hers and those of the man named Mark.

When she joined Colin in the living room, he had the lights low, a bowl of popcorn and two glasses of wine on the coffee table and was dressed in nothing more than a pair of cotton plaid lounge pants. Gracious the man looked good.

"Wine. The perfect thing after a day like today." She sat on the opposite end of the sofa and grabbed one of the glasses.

"I even found a movie in your stack of DVDs. Something called P.S. I Love You."

"One of my favorites." She peered at him over the rim of her glass. The man was up to something. "Tomorrow, I need to research the two names we were given at the college."

"No work talk. You need time off. Morning will come fast enough." He pressed the TV remote. "Come closer. You're too far away."

"I'm fine where I am."

"It'll be hard to share the popcorn." He sat the bowl in his lap.

The man played dirty for sure. Sitting that close to him was asking for trouble. "I can get another bowl."

"Are you afraid of me, Cassidy?" His eyes darkened.

She snorted. "No way. You're the softy in this partnership. The good cop. A real boy scout."

"Let me show you how bad I can be." His brogue deepened. "Let me help you forget your pain. Snuggle close and watch this chick flick with me."

What could it hurt? She could use the distraction. Sitting next to him, smelling his heady cologne, breathing in…him. She scooted closer and let him put his arm around her shoulders. "You said you wouldn't be a demanding roommate."

"You make it hard in some cases." He grinned down at her. "The sight of you in that red dress did things to my mind. I can not be held responsible."

"Stop it." She slapped his chest, freezing when he held her hand there. Heat radiated through her palm. Her gaze clashed with his. Before she did something stupid, like kiss him, she gulped her wine.

He moved her hand holding the wine glass from her mouth. She jerked. Wine spilled down his naked chest.

Colin jumped to his feet, almost tossing her to the floor. "Oh, that's cold."

"I'm sorry." She dashed to the kitchen and grabbed a handful of paper towels. Hurrying back, she dabbed at his chest.

"It's fine. I'll take a shower." He chuckled and strolled away, muttering something about taking her mind off unpleasant things.

Oh, he did that all right. She laughed softly, refilled her wine glass, and settled back on the sofa. The man was definitely a distraction. Funny how that didn't seem to upset her as much as it had at first. It was nice having him around.

She glanced to where Rosie watched them. "A little bark when things start to get heated would be nice, my girl. You're supposed to be here to protect me." And she definitely needed protecting from Colin.

Her ears twitched.

"Seriously, us girls have to stick together." She got to her feet, motioned for Rosie to follow her, and headed upstairs to bed where she would be safe from the distraction of handsome men.

~

Cassidy's eyes popped open. A horrible moaning came from Colin's room. "Stay," she whispered to Rosie as she got out of bed.

Barefoot, she plodded to the room next door, pushed the door open, and peered inside. "Colin?"

He thrashed, tangled in the sheets. She rushed to his side and placed a hand on his shoulder. "Colin, you're having a nightmare."

Moonlight streamed through the open curtains, highlighting his features. Perspiration coated his chest and face. He gripped her arm, his eyes wide. "I didn't mean to."

"Shh. I know." She had no idea what he meant, but sat on the side of his bed and smoothed a dark curl away from his face. "It's going to be okay."

"Never. I can never forget." His eyes closed. The sheet he covered with slipped, revealing a taut stomach and the fact Colin preferred to sleep in the nude.

Oh, boy. It also became evident he was talking in his sleep. What should she do? She tried to remember whether she'd read that you are to wake up the person having the nightmare or try to comfort them in their sleep? Since he didn't seem as if he would do harm to himself, Cassidy chose comfort.

She pulled the sheet higher on his chest and caressed his cheek. Stubble rasped against her hand. A tear slid down his cheek. She leaned forward and brushed it away with her lips.

And found herself flat on her back with Colin on top of her. His lips claimed hers, his hands running up and down her body, lifting her shirt.

For a moment, she contemplated giving in. No. Going through with what he was offering would complicate their relationship beyond repair.

"Colin, wake up." She pushed against him. "Colin!" Her palm stung from the force of her slap.

~

Colin jerked awake and rolled off Cassidy. "I'm sorry. I'm so sorry." He lowered his legs off the bed and buried his face in his hands.

"You were asleep." Her voice held a definite chill as she sat up.

Whether from his forcing himself on her or because he'd withdrawn, he was afraid to find out which had made her angry. He'd woken in time. "Why are you in my room?"

"You had a nightmare." The rustling of the bedsheet told him she got up.

"I have them a lot."

"This is the first time I've heard you."

He turned his head as she stood in front of him.

"Colin, look at me."

He sighed and glanced up. Her hair was mussed, her lips swollen. He shook his head. "How's that for a distraction?"

"Don't get crude." She put a hand on his arm. "It was a mistake. Are you all right?"

After what he'd almost done, she was worried about him. Asleep or not, he'd betrayed her trust and a vow he'd made to himself a long time ago. Never get physically entangled with a partner. He'd come too close to stepping over that line.

He shrugged off her touch. "Please go." He turned away so he wouldn't have to see the pain flickering across her face.

"All right." Her soft words tore at him. "Please don't sleep in the nude anymore."

He didn't get up until her heard her bedroom door close. Then, he flopped back on the bed and flung his arm across his eyes. What a fool!

How would he face her? He groaned and rolled onto his side, hugging a pillow to his chest. *I'm sorry, Cassidy.*

~

Well, that was a first, Cassidy thought as she slammed her door. No one had ever regretted making out with her before or sent her packing from their room. Not that there had been many men. Just one in college and she had sent *him* away when she'd discovered she was one of many notches on his bedpost. She'd vowed to stay celibate after that, but Colin's vulnerability had shot down every defensive brick in the wall she'd built around herself.

"Now what?" she asked Rosie. "Do I pretend it never happened?" She couldn't. What an idiot she was.

If they were members of a larger police force, she'd request a new partner. As it was, they were stuck with each other.

She lay on her bed and stared through the dark at the ceiling. What a predicament. Shame washed over her like a cold winter rain. She shouldn't have kissed him. Stroking his hair had seemed to be working. Why had she gotten so close?

Rosie growled deep in her throat.

Cassidy shot to a sitting position and reached for the gun on her nightstand.

Something crashed through her bedroom window.

She dove to the floor, scooting under the heavy bed as something exploded. "Rosie!"

The dog yelped and scurried to her side.

Cassidy slapped out burning fur and fought to see through the smoke.

"Cassidy!"

"Under here."

A hand grabbed her and yanked her out and to her feet. "Let's go." Colin dragged her along, Rosie following.

"What happened?"

"Looks like a pipe bomb."

"My house!" Cassidy grabbed a fire extinguisher from the wall and headed back to her room.

"I'll do it. Get back." Dressed again in his plaid pants, but barefoot, Colin aimed the extinguisher at the wall opposite Cassidy's bed.

With one hand on Rosie's collar and her tee shirt pulled over her nose, she watched through streaming eyes as Colin put out the fire. When that was done, she retrieved her cell phone and called 911.

"Stay close by me. We're going downstairs." Colin gripped her arm. Gone was the tender lover, replaced by a grim Scottish warrior.

In the kitchen, he ordered her to sit at the bar, then proceeded to pick slivers of glass from the bottom of his feet. "He hasn't wanted you dead before. What changed?"

"It was risky to think a pipe bomb would kill me. How did he know I was in my room?" She shrugged.

"What. Changed?" He enunciated each word.

"Us. That's what changed." She glared at him. "Is that what you wanted to hear?"

"How does he know? Think. You have to be aware of everything happening around you. All the time."

She quieted, running through each room in her mind. Her eyes widened. "Your curtains were open. He watched us."

~

How dare she! Draco gunned his engine and sped into the night. His precious girl was soiled now.

She was no longer any good to him. Not for the purpose he wanted anyway. How could she lead his followers when he was gone? They needed someone pure in mind, if not in body. Someone like him. After Maureen, he'd had no other women. He thought his daughter kept the same values. What if she didn't share his blood? What if Maureen had not been the nice girl she'd seemed?

Cassidy was no better than the others he targeted. Using her pretty face and lovely body to lure others into her web. He needed to find out for sure whether he had fathered her. If not, his plans would have to change.

The Scot had been sleeping! Deep in the throes of a nightmare. She'd taken advantage of him and needed to be punished. The pipe bomb was a warning.

Maybe her partner had led her on earlier in the day like Maureen had toyed with his affections a long time ago. Let her know he was open to her charms. Perhaps he wasn't innocent in their night time romp. He'd have to be eliminated. No more games.

Draco would still lure Cassidy to his clutches. Somehow, he'd get her DNA and have a test run. Any fool could purchase the kit off the internet. He couldn't make further plans until he knew for certain.

He sped home, closing the grey Lexus in the garage. He needed a consoling drink. He needed to kill someone!

In the house, he poured a double shot of whiskey and headed for his office and his list of names. He'd said he'd leave the killing to others, but in this case...

He chose a woman who had laughed in his face at a bar, calling him a freak. All he'd wanted to do was buy her a drink, have a little conversation. He'd planned on saving her for later, but tomorrow was not her lucky day.

12

Wrapped in a blanket too thick for the summer evening, Cassidy watched as Colin, still shirtless, spoke with the FBI agents and firemen raced into her house to make sure the fire danger was over. Colin had known when he'd asked how The Dragon knew about what had almost transpired. He'd wanted her to come to the same conclusion.

Whatever sweetness might have been from Colin's kisses and tender endearments had been sullied, tossed into the dirt and stomped on. It was for the best. It shouldn't have happened and the consequences were now more dire than she would have imagined. The target on her back was as big as the Ozark mountains.

She glanced at the trees bordering her property. Was he watching? Wanting to view his handiwork? The temptation to go and see was strong. But, she stayed perched on the hood of her car. Heading off alone would be stupid. There were times she might be impulsive, but stupidity was not a trait she wanted others to think of her as having.

Sarah Robertson, reporter and all around nuisance, approached Colin with a wolf whistle. He said something to hear, leaving her with a scowl on her face, and donned a shirt handed to him by Agent Ingram, then marched Cassidy's way. "Are you all right?"

"I'm fine. The house is fine. Everything's great."

He sat next to her, his weight popping the hood. "Don't sulk. There isn't time for a pity party."

She glared. "I never feel sorry for myself. It's a wasted emotion."

"We could see you sulking from the front porch." He straightened the blanket around her.

"It's too hot."

"You might be in shock."

"I'm not that weak. Nothing is damaged but my room." And her pride. "I can deal with that."

"Are you up to finding and interviewing the other two college students who didn't return to the party the night your mother was attacked? The fire department will clear the house soon and we can grab some sleep. I'll take the sofa."

"No, you stay in the guest room." She wouldn't get a lick of sleep in that bed. "I've slept there plenty of times watching TV. You'll hang off the edge. I'll call someone to repair my bedroom."

"They'll have to be checked out by the FBI before we'll allow them in," Agent Ingram said, approaching the jeep. "I'll have Agent West find someone. Glad to see you're doing fine."

"Except for the fact this perp stays one step ahead of us." She shrugged off the blanket and slid from the jeep's hood. "What do we do? Wait for him to come for me again?"

"He'll slip up eventually." Ingram clapped her on the shoulder. "In the meantime, keep hunting." He flashed a thin-lipped smile and left to join the other agents.

Without glancing at Colin, Cassidy headed for the house to prepare a bed on the sofa, knowing without asking that Colin would sleep on the floor next to her.

~

Surprised that she had actually slept, Cassidy woke to the now familiar smell of breakfast and brewing coffee. She stretched, popping the kinks from her back and made a vain attempt to smooth her hair into place.

Colin, frying pan in hand, gave her a smile from the doorway that didn't quite meet his eyes. Those were still shadowed with shame.

She sighed and returned his pasted on smile. Two could pretend nothing had happened, but there would come a day when they had to talk about what had almost happened in detail. Especially if they were to continue being partners. Nothing would be the same between them. They'd almost crossed a line she'd promised herself to never step over. She had no intention of leaving her home. If they couldn't work together as professionals, he would have to be the one to leave.

"Omelets," Colin said. "You have time to take a quick shower if you want. I took mine earlier."

"I want." She bounded up the stairs and through her room smelling strongly of smoke. Someone had taped plastic over the shattered window. The opposite wall was burned black, along with most of the bedding. Refusing to let the sight break her, Cassidy moved to the bathroom where, hopefully, a hot shower would clear her head and help her forget the night before.

When she'd finished and dressed in her customary baggy clothes, no suit today, she joined Colin in the kitchen.

His eyebrows rose at her outfit, but he wisely held his tongue and slid a plate full of omelet and bacon toward her. "I found the addresses for Daniel Haler and Vince Smith, so we're ready to go once you've eaten."

"Did you sleep at all last night?" She cut her fork into the fluffy omelet.

"Not much," he muttered, turning away.

They ate in silence, the tension thicker than an autumn fog rolling across a lake. Cassidy tried not to take peeks at the man sitting next to her, and failed. She wanted to tell him it was okay. What had almost happened wasn't the end of the world. Just an unfortunate mistake that, if they'd gone through with it, could have been dealt with.

She finished her breakfast, set her plate in the sink, and grabbed her badge and gun. "I'm ready."

Colin nodded and followed suit, then set the alarm on the front door and followed Cassidy to the jeep. "Who's driving?"

"I will." She climbed into the driver's seat.

"Haler lives in Little Rock, Smith in Conway."

"Smith first then." She backed the jeep from the drive and headed down Interstate 40. "Are we going to his home or work?"

"I don't know where they work. I'm hoping neighbors can tell us." He rubbed his unshaven chin. "You don't need to make aimless conversation, Cassidy. I'm over my temper tantrum."

"Good."

~

He chuckled wryly. Cassidy seemed determined to pretend nothing had changed between them, so he'd follow her lead. If he didn't, guilt would consume him. He couldn't work efficiently under those circumstances. "Take the second exit," he said, glancing at his GPS.

"What's with the nightmares?"

"I don't like talking about them." He adopted the cocky attitude that always made her stop talking. "Of course, you coming to my room and all helped erase some of that."

"It won't work."

"What won't?"

"Making a joke of it. Tell me about your nightmare." Her hands tightened on the steering wheel.

She was like a bulldog. He glanced out the window. "I shot an innocent woman."

"Okay, I wasn't expecting that. What happened?"

"Do we really have to do this?"

"I think so."

He grinned. "Not going to come comfort me anymore?"

"If you don't stop with the jokes, I'm going to punch you in the throat." She whipped the wheel to the side and swerved into the parking lot of a grocery store before facing him. "I am not a pain killer for you. I am not a nurse maid. I am not your comforter, although I lost myself for a minute. I am your partner, and I want to know what your nightmares are about so I can find a more healthy way of helping you."

Ouch. "On a professional basis."

"Yes." Her look could cut steel. "Sometimes, talking about these things actually help them stop. Have you seen a counselor?"

"Many times." He didn't believe in them, which is why they probably didn't work. "We had a hostage situation in New York shortly after I arrived in the states and entered the police force. A man was holding two women and a small child inside a dress boutique. One of them was his girlfriend and her daughter, the other the store clerk. My sergeant ordered me to take the shot. I squeezed the trigger right as the man pulled the woman tighter against him. The shot went through him and into her, killing them both."

"That wasn't your fault." She made a move to put a hand on his arm, then drew back.

Now, she was afraid to touch him. Way to go, MacKenzie. "I should have waited."

"You didn't know. You were following a direct order."

"Are you always going to make excuses for me?" He narrowed his eyes. "I was asleep, I didn't know what I was doing, I almost forced myself on you, I didn't know he was going to pull the woman close? Stop making excuses for me."

"Fine. It's all your fault." She drove back onto the road. "Maybe you need to learn to forgive yourself."

The load was too heavy. Forgiving himself didn't seem harsh enough in light of the things he'd done. "Can we forget personal conversation and keep things strictly professional? It'll be a heck of a lot safer."

She rolled her eyes. "That was my intention all along."

~

Draco strolled into the bar, Mary trailing a few feet behind him. If he wanted the woman off his back, he needed to let her finish deleting her enemies.

She pointed out the target, a pretty blond around the age of twenty-five sitting alone at the polished mahogany bar. She was turned to face the men playing pool, her emerald slip of a dress sitting high on her thighs.

He knew her type. He'd approach her, ask to buy her a drink, and get laughed at. Then, he'd pester her until she made the excuse to use the restroom, where he'd grab her, drag her through a back door and turn her over to Mary. So simple these pretty people. So predictable.

"Hey, pretty lady. Can I buy you a drink?" He was careful to keep the scarred side of his face away from her. Let her think him handsome for a few seconds more.

She tilted her head, a sliver of a smile on her glossy lips. "Sure. Chardonnay, please."

Motioning to the bartender, he placed the order, then faced her full on, knowing how the scar twisted his lips on the one side. "Do you come here often?"

Her eyes widened. "Um, no. Excuse me. I'll be right back."

Just as planned, she headed for the glowing red sign marked restrooms.

Just once, he'd like to know what it felt like for a woman not to look at him with revulsion in her eyes. He paid the tab, took the glass of wine, and followed Mary's prey, motioning for the other woman to follow.

He dropped a tablet into the wine and waited. "You forgot your drink," he said, when the woman emerged.

"Oh, thank you, but I must decline. My boyfriend…"

"One of those playing pool?" Right. Liar.

"Yes." She smiled. "I really must get back."

"Please take your drink. No hard feelings." He held out the glass. "You can at least spare me a few minutes since I bought it for you."

"I...suppose." She took a sip, then another, as if by hurrying, she could rid herself of his company. She swayed on her feet. "Oh, I must have drank it too fast."

"Here, let me help you. No strings attached." He clubbed her on the side of the head, then propped one shoulder under one arm while Mary moved forward to take the other.

They helped their victim outside and into the trunk of Mary's twelve-year-old Dodge Charger. "You make it look so easy," Mary said.

"It is easy. You need only learn to read people. Who is this woman to you?"

"My father's youngest daughter by his new trophy wife. She's done nothing but point out how much better she is than me. Thinner, more attractive, more successful. I can't wait to rid the world of her." Mary slammed the trunk.

"Be patient and take care."

"Aren't you coming?"

Draco shook his head as he slid behind into the driver's seat of his car. "I'll be sure to watch the video. You should know what to do by now." With a toss of his hand, he drove away. He couldn't babysit the woman forever. She knew the consequences if she messed up. Either he would dispose of her or turn her over to the authorities. Either way, she'd no longer be his concern. He had bigger things to take care of.

13

Cassidy followed Colin's directions to a large apartment complex on the edge of Conway. From the looks of the place, Vince Smith had fallen on hard times.

Wood trim in need of paint, white siding grayed from the weather, a pool thick with slime, and more rusty automobiles than should be in one place. Weeds claimed every patch of ground that sported a bit of dirt. The sign out front stated luxury apartments for lease. Must be a lot less.

Side-by-side, she and Colin climbed stairs to the third floor. Cassidy stood off to one side while Colin rapped sharply on the splintered door. The man who answered had more tattooed skin than not. A scar, covered by a snake tattoo, disappeared down his shirt.

"Vince Smith?" Colin flashed his badge. "Mind if we ask you a few questions?"

"What about?" The man reeked of cigarette smoke.

"Something that happened at college a long time ago. The attack of Maureen Monroe ring a bell?"

"That night haunts me." He stepped aside and waved them into an apartment so clean Cassidy had to take another look outside to make sure she hadn't entered an alternate dimension. "Have a seat," he said. "Y'all want a soda or water?"

"No, thank you." Cassidy perched on the edge of a dark brown leather sofa.

Colin took a chair across from her.

Vince sat in a chair angled to face the one Colin had chosen. "That was such a long time ago, man." He rubbed both hands down his face.

"Did you know Maureen?" Cassidy kept her gaze glued to his face.

"Yeah, we went out a time or two. Sweet girl." He shook his head. "She wasn't much of a partier, but wasn't a prude either. She could have fun…when it was called for."

"Did you see who she left the party with?"

"Nah, I was drunk as a skunk. Spent most of my college life that way. Ended up getting dropped from my classes. Me and my buddies heard her scream, then some guys carried her out of the trees. She was covered in blood." He shuddered.

"Was there anyone there you didn't know? Anyone who stood out?" Cassidy glanced at Colin, glad to see him taking notes, then transferred her attention back to Vince.

"A lot of people." He frowned. "It was one of those mixer things where students could get to know each other. We had Freshmen to Senior there. There's no way I could have seen everyone." He drummed his fingers on the arm of his chair. "There was this one guy. Pretty good-looking, I guess. He kept going from girl to girl, flirting and offering them drinks."

"Can you describe him?" Cassidy leaned closer.

"Dark hair, blue eyes, maybe. When he came up to the girl I was hanging with, I run him off."

"Did he talk to Maureen?"

"Yeah." His eyes widened. "I could tell she was only being polite. Wasn't really into the guy. I looked over there a couple of times, just in case she needed me to get rid of him, but they were laughing and seemed to be getting along. When they disappeared, I didn't think much of it. Man, do you think it was him? Could I have saved her?"

"You were one of the male students who didn't return to the party when Maureen was found. Where were you?"

"Passed out with the girl I was hanging with. After seeing Maureen, finding out what happened, well, I drank a lot more." He hung his head. "I had to erase the image of her, you know? I'll never forgive myself if I could have done something."

In his condition, Cassidy doubted he could have done much. She handed him a business card. "Please call if you think of anything else. Anything at all that might help us find this guy."

He took the card. "Why are you looking after all these years?"

"We believe he may be responsible in the death of another young woman." She stood and offered her hand. "Thank you for your time."

He shook her hand. "I'm sorry I couldn't do more."

They at least had a description of sorts. Not that they could take the word of a drunken college student twenty-five years after the fact, but it was more than they had when they arrived. That, and the fact her mother might have left willingly with her attacker.

"Do you know whether they did a tox screen on my mother?" she asked Colin once they stepped outside. "What if this man she was laughing with slipped her something?"

"The same thought occurred to me. I didn't see anything in her file, though."

Since she hadn't been killed, most likely the screen hadn't been scheduled. Either that or her mother hadn't gone to be tested. She sighed and climbed back into the jeep.

Their next stop was an expensive community in North Little Rock. They pulled into the long drive and parked next to a red Ford convertible.

Cassidy squelched a bit of car envy and led the way to the front door. She pressed the bell and waited. When several minutes passed, she knocked. "Where to now?"

Colin dug through the mail in the mailbox. "He's probably at work. We need to find out where that is. Nothing here." He replaced the mail.

"Can I help you?" An elderly man came around the corner of the house, a shovel in his hand. "The Halers are working."

Colin flashed his badge. "We need to speak with Mr. Haler. Do you have the address of his job?"

He shook his head. "It's something, something, Haler. A law firm."

Colin grinned. "We'll find it from that. Thank you." He started to take Cassidy's elbow, then dropped his hand.

Good grief. It wasn't like touching her would burn him or anything. Oh, that's right. He didn't need his painkiller right now. Well, next time he had a nightmare, she'd yell loudly from the doorway! No more getting too close. She was the one who would get burned.

~

Colin rolled his head on stiff shoulders and wished for a good night's sleep. He had a prescription from the last counselor he'd seen, but after Cassidy's nighttime visit, then the pipe bomb, he needed to be alert. Hopefully, he'd sleep that night from sheer exhaustion.

"Haler looks like he does well for himself," he said, studying the brick two-story office building in front of him. "Funny how people in the same class at college can take such different routes."

Cassidy made a noise in her throat and pushed open the double glass doors. "Let's hope he has a minute to speak with us."

Colin shot out an arm to hold the door open, then followed Cassidy into the plush waiting room. Their shoes clipped across the marble floor.

A receptionist smiled at them from behind a oak desk. “Welcome to Larson, Moore, and Haler. How may I help you?”

Colin showed his badge again, thinking he might as well wear it around his neck. “We need to speak with Daniel Haler, please.”

“Let me see if he is available.” Her smile never wavered as she punched buttons on her phone. “Mr. Haler, the police are here to see you. May I send them in? Thank you, sir.” She beamed up at them. “He’s busy.”

“Tough.” Cassidy glanced at a sign. “We’ll show ourselves in.” She marched down a long hall.

Colin shrugged at the lovely receptionist, smiled, and followed the Bull Dog. “You get more with sugar than vinegar.”

“I’ve heard that.” She continued to the elevators and pressed the button for the fourth floor. “You can remain the good cop. I’m comfortable with my role.”

The elevator doors opened and they stepped inside. Immediately, tension filled the space as the doors closed.

Colin kept his gaze locked on the numbers flashing above the buttons. He would have to find a way to be alone with Cassidy without feeling like a boy with a crush. One who had snuck a kiss while playing Truth or Dare. He remained still while the doors opened and she stepped out, then followed her to the right.

A brass plate on a glass door announced they'd found Daniel Haler. Cassidy shoved open the door, bypassed a wide-eyed girl behind a counter and marched into the man's office. "We're Detectives Monroe and MacKenzie. Thank you for seeing us."

The man's face darkened. "I said I was busy."

Colin stepped forward to diffuse a situation that could spiral out of control. "Sir, this is important. We only want a few minutes of your time." He closed the door and took a seat across from Haler, motioning for Cassidy to do the same.

"We're here about an assault on a Maureen Monroe that happened while you were at college." Cassidy tossed a business card on his desk.

"I had nothing to do with that." The man scooted his chair back a foot. "I barely knew her."

"Where did you go that night?" Gone was the nice officer who had questioned Smith. Cassidy was sharp as nails and about as friendly as a pit bull.

Colin bit back a grin. This was the woman he'd met over the first victim's body. This hard-nosed partner he could deal with.

"I was at the party." Haler's brows drew together.

"After Maureen was brought to the on-campus clinic, you were one of the few men not spotted again for several days."

His gaze flicked around the room. "I...don't know where I was."

"Do you have any scars, Mr. Haler?" Cassidy gave him a shark-like grin. "From a knife, perhaps?"

"No, nothing, I swear." Terror filled his eyes.

"Do you mind visiting the restroom with Detective MacKenzie? Or would you prefer a search warrant?"

"I have nothing to hide." He lunged to his feet. "Fine." He unbuttoned his shirt. "I was stabbed a few years ago by a disgruntled client. You can check my medical records. I pressed charges. What's this all about anyway." He fixed his shirt. "That girl's attack happened a long time ago."

"Sir." Colin held up his hand to halt Cassidy from further questioning. "We believe her attacker may have recently killed another woman. Anything you can tell us will be greatly appreciated."

He settled back in his chair. "I was there as a spy." He shook his head. "The dean wanted to know who brought drugs to the parties on campus. I'd drink, then go in the bushes and throw up, then start the process all over again. I was purging when I heard a girl scream. I didn't know at the time that it was Maureen. When I parted the bushes, a guy was running away holding his face. Blood was everywhere. I got sick for real and fell in my vomit. By the time I was conscious, it was all over and she was being cared for."

Colin glanced at Cassidy. Hope shone in her eyes.

"He was holding his face?" she asked.

"Yeah, like this." Haler cupped his cheek. "That's all I could tell. Oh, and he had dark hair."

Cassidy jumped to her feet and reached across the desk to shake his hand. "Thank you." She took a deep breath and left the room.

Colin shrugged at Haler and joined her in the hall. "Talk about doing a one eighty."

"We now know any injury my mother caused him was to the face. I say that's a huge step forward. Now, we can check hospital records of that night without questioning every single person stabbed that night."

"Do you get many stabbings around here?"

"We didn't get much of anything around here...until recently. Not in Clear Springs, anyway." She pressed the button on the elevator again.

The tension was somewhat relieved as Cassidy continued to talk of what they'd learned. Excitement laced her words. "We can get the FBI to help us track down knife victims and interview the names we find. I mean, I'd like to have a go at all the names we find, but the interviews will go a lot faster with five people instead of two." She glanced up at him and fell silent.

He hadn't meant for her to catch him looking at her as if she were the most beautiful thing he'd ever seen. He hadn't wanted her to see in his eyes how he was growing to feel about her. Especially after the other night. He cleared his throat and looked away.

"I think having help is a good thing." He closed his eyes and prayed for strength.

14

The conference room echoed as five people made phone calls to hospitals and clinics within a fifty mile radius of the college. Cassidy set her pencil down and stretched. It would have definitely taken just her and Colin forever to go down the list. Once they had their suspects, she prayed she would be the one who got her mother's attacker. She rubbed her hands together. She'd love to get her hands on him.

Colin looked up from his phone and laughed. "You look pleased with yourself."

"Plotting revenge." She smiled. "Two more locations on my list." She reached down and scratched behind Rosie's ears.

"I'm finished. I have five names to visit."

She frowned. It wasn't a competition, yet she looked at it as one. She quickly made the remaining calls, came up with zip, and then stood, glancing at Ingram. "Do we take the names we each have?"

"You two take yours. We'll take the rest. No one interviews anyone alone," he said. "Understood?" He cast a stern dark-eyed gaze around the table. "In fact, I think it wise that the two of you take Weston with you. The danger to Monroe is too great."

They all nodded and gathered their things.

While Cassidy didn't need a babysitter, having a third person around would help keep things less tense between her and Colin. Maybe her and Weston could be friends. She could use a girlfriend. Especially the other night. Hashing over her feelings for Colin, sharing a bottle of wine, talking about...what did close friends talk about?

She studied the cool, but beautiful features of the FBI agent. She didn't look like she was in the market for a friend. Smith and Weston rarely spoke, unlike Ingram.

"We'll take the rented SUV," Weston said. "The killer knows Monroe's vehicle. Knocking on the door and flashing our badges is all the announcement we need." She marched out of the building ahead of them.

Cassidy tossed Colin a surprised look. "Do you think she's upset to play bodyguard?"

He shrugged. "Let's just get through the day." He leaned close, giving her a teasing whiff of his musky cologne. "I think she has a thing for Ingram."

"Really?" Cassidy glanced at the other two men. "Interesting."

"Maybe we can get her to open up to us." He winked and held the front door open.

Her heart did a somersault. Relieved to not feel the usual tension between them, she hurried to the SUV and got in the backseat with Rosie. The dog had found an empty spot in Cassidy's heart. She couldn't imagine going anywhere without her now.

The moment Colin's seatbelt clicked into place, Weston began barking orders. "I do the talking. I knock, announce myself, and enter any residence first. There are vests in the back. Each of you are to wear one. Do not pull your weapon for any reason unless I pull mine first."

"What if the suspect fires first and you're down?" Cassidy couldn't help the jab. "Can we think for ourselves then?"

Weston glared at her through the rearview mirror. "Keep your wits and sarcasm. Today could very well be the day we catch a killer."

Cassidy squelched any thought of them being friends. Oh, well. She had Rosie. She didn't need anyone else. Instead, she stared at the back of Colin's head and thought of things that might be possible...if she let her guard down. Which she had no intention of doing.

"Remember. I take the lead," Weston reminded them as they pulled in front of a well-maintained home built in the 1950s. She cast a warning look over her shoulder at Cassidy, then exited the vehicle.

Cassidy told Rosie to stay and followed the agent and Colin to the front door. She stood a few feet away from Weston and peered through a crack in the curtains. "Television is on, but I don't see anyone."

"Get away from the window." Weston shook her head. "Bullets shatter glass."

Cassidy sighed. She wasn't an imbecile, but unless they were very lucky and the killer was actually at home with open curtains, she didn't think they were in much danger.

They were just turning to leave when an African American man answered the door. A knife scar ran from his temple past his eye.

"FBI." Weston showed her badge. "We'd like to ask you a few questions."

"I've not had any trouble in years," the man said. "Ask what you want from out here."

"How did you get that scar?"

"Gang fight." He crossed his arms. "But I don't live that life no more."

"He doesn't fit the profile." Weston thanked him for his time and headed back to the SUV.

It went that way for most of the day. One after the other they ticked off the names on their list as non-suspects.

Frustration gnawed at Cassidy the way Rosie chewed on a rawhide. The killer had to be close. He had to have a scar down his face. While all the men they'd interviewed were the right age, it was obvious most of them weren't the killer. Half of them had never gone to college and had received their wounds in fights and accidents.

They stopped for lunch at a fast food Mexican place and ate in the car. Colin had been unusually quiet the first half of the day.

"I have two names left on my list. One is a man in his mid-fifties," he said. "The age is right. He received thirty stitches on the left side of his face twenty-five years ago. The other man is also in his fifties and the scar is along the neck. He almost bled out, according to the ER records. My guess…we visit the first guy. Maureen may have wounded her attacker, but I just don't feel like she could have gotten in a good enough whack to almost kill him."

Weston turned in her seat. "I've read your file. You have good instincts. Both of you do. So, if that's what your gut is telling you, that's where we'll go next. I need to check in with Agent Ingram." She exited the car and punched numbers into her cell phone. Immediately a grin spread across her face.

"So she can smile," Cassidy said. "I was starting to wonder."

"You don't reign as Ice Queen anymore. Not with her around."

"Who calls me that?" She stabbed a piece of carne asada with her plastic fork."

"Everyone. I did, too, until…" he sighed. "Now, you're the Bull Dog."

"Ugh. I prefer Ice Queen."

"Sorry, but you've been knocked off your frigid throne." He leaned forward and peered closer at Weston. "Something's wrong."

The agent slid back into the driver's seat. "We have another body. Interviews will have to wait." She cursed, thrust the vehicle into drive and sped down the highway.

~

"This isn't The Dragon's work." Colin stared at the knife wounds to the victim's face. "He would never mar her beauty."

"One of his followers?" Cassidy squatted next to the body. "There has to be either followers or copycats either doing his bidding or with agendas of their own."

Which would make it extremely hard to find and arrest them all. He knelt next to his partner and studied the body close up. "She reeks of alcohol. We need to visit the bars in the area. See if anyone recognizes her." He glanced around the area. "No purse."

Cassidy tapped the woman's hip. "I think her ID is in her underwear." She shrugged at Colin's glance. "Where else is she supposed to carry it? Turn around."

He averted his gaze while she fished out the woman's ID. "Same last name as one of our other victims."

"Sisters?" He took the driver's license. "We might have finally gotten a break."

"Find a common enemy." Cassidy pushed to her feet. "Do that first or interview scar face."

"That's cruel."

"It's nothing compared to what I'm going to do with the man when we catch him." She stepped aside while the emergency personnel zipped the body into a bag. "I think he distracts us with dead bodies to keep us from getting too close."

"How so?" Colin leaned against the side of the SUV.

"Well..." She took her bottom lip between her teeth.

Colin took a deep breath to halt the effect of what even that small gesture did to him.

"We find out that he's scarred in the face and start interviewing. We find a body—" She held up a hand to stop him from saying anything. "I know this woman was killed before we started knocking on doors. The point is...he's one step ahead all the time. He's smart enough to know we're low on law enforcement personnel and that dropping crumbs like some perverted Hansel and Gretel, he can keep us from zeroing in on one thing."

"She's right." Ingram joined them. "I've called for reinforcements. We're stretched too thin. They should arrive in the morning. I know all this is out of your jurisdiction, Monroe, but I appreciate the hard work."

"Why not Colin's jurisdiction?"

"He's been a detective a lot longer and was almost recruited by the FBI." He gave Cassidy an indulgent smile. "You're learning on one case what it took us to learn over several."

"Lucky me." She exhaled sharply. "Let's use those computer skills of yours, Colin, and watch this latest video before we knock on more doors. We can visit the bar later."

"Yes, boss." He grinned at Ingram. "At least she's pretty."

The agent laughed. "Lucky man. You've got both the women."

There was only one he wanted, though, and she shied away like a skittish horse if his hand so much as brushed hers. He chuckled along with the other man, hiding his feelings, then left to join the women.

Several minutes later he'd located the video. "See how the killer stands? It's definitely the same woman who killed this victim's relative."

"Why haven't we seen videos other than The Dragon and this woman?" Weston asked. "Do you think she's his only accomplice?"

"No. There were the ones who set off the bomb on Main Street, then the man pretending to be a photographer. There's no telling how many followers he has." Colin kept his gaze glued at the screen. "Last time, it was almost as if she was performing for someone. I don't think our dragon is there this time."

"She's flying solo?" Cassidy leaned closer, her hair brushing Colin's cheek.

He took a deep whiff of floral-scented shampoo. "That's why she's taking her time with the face."

"That looks like a scalpel." Cassidy tapped the screen. "She could work in the medical field."

"We can't call every doctor's office in the state of Arkansas. We need something else to narrow our search." He scanned the edges of the video feed. Trees, trees, and...wait a minute. He squinted. "Does that look like a car in the bushes?"

Soon he was flanked on the other side by Weston. If he wasn't so enamored by his partner, he'd be in any man's dream. He shook off his thoughts. "A dark blue sedan?"

“I can’t make out the license plate.” Weston straightened. “Forward to this email. I’ll have our technicians take a look. Maybe they can zoom in enough to read the numbers.”

A mere second later the video was soaring through cyber space. They may have gotten another break.

He crooked both arms to the women. “Let’s go catch a killer.”

15

"This is it." Cassidy glanced at the name on the paper, Russell Ball, and the expensive looking apartments in front of them.

"Same orders as before," Weston said as she marched through the double glass doors of the building.

Cassidy was getting tired of her bossy attitude. Counting to ten, she followed the agent into the elevator and pressed the button for the third floor. A penthouse apartment, at least in these parts.

When the elevator stopped, Colin ushered the women out first. "Let's make this quick. It's been a long day and we still need to talk to the bartender."

"Quick *and* thorough," Weston pointed out.

"That's right, Colin." Cassidy smirked, teasing. "Remember your priorities."

"Yes, ma'am." He grinned, sending her insides quivering.

"You two stop playing around." Weston pressed the doorbell and held her badge to the peep hole. "FBI."

The door cracked open and blue eyes peered out. "One second, please." They heard the sounds of a chain being removed and the door swung open.

Russell Ball's scar started right below his left eye and into the curve of his lips, twisting them into a joker-style grin. "Come in." He waved his arm in a grand gesture.

Cassidy glanced around a modern, immaculate apartment. If not for dishes containing the remnants of the man's meal, she'd doubt anyone lived there. She returned the man's stare, keeping her features impassive at his disfigurement.

"I'm Agent Weston. This is Detective Monroe and Detective MacKenzie. I see we've disturbed your dinner and will be as brief as possible." She flinched and averted her eyes from his face.

"Have a seat." Ball's eyes narrowed as he motioned to the pale gray sofa. "I was finished eating. How may I help you?"

Weston sat on the edge of the sofa and leaned her elbows on her knees. "Let's start with how you got that scar?" She swallowed hard.

"That's a bit rude, but all right." His smile faded. "A terrible car accident many years ago."

Weston flipped through pages on her clipboard. "I have no record of you being in a car accident. Only that you went to an Urgent Care facility twenty-five years ago for what they described as a knife wound."

He shrugged. "The facility was overworked that night. An honest mistake."

"Did you know a Maureen Monroe?"

He thought, placing a finger on his lips. "I don't believe so."

"From college? A frat party, maybe?"

"Definitely not. I stayed to myself in college. My education was more important than chasing skirts. My college transcripts will attest to that." His gaze flicked to Cassidy.

"Mr. Ball." Cassidy took a deep breath. "On the night you received that wound, a woman was viciously attacked. A woman that happens to be my mother. She cut her attacker. You are one of three men who were at the party, but not seen again after her attack. Where did you go?"

He scratched his chin. "You're investigating an attack that happened twenty-five years ago? How should I know where I went?"

"You strike me as an intelligent man," she said. "I think you know very well where you were. An attack on a woman would leave an impression on anyone."

"Fine." He bent and hung his hands between his knees. "I was at the party. I left to snort a line of coke and passed out next to the pool. I can't let this mar my record. I'm a successful businessman."

"Do you have an alibi?"

"Detective Monroe." He stood. "When a student of my caliber does something like that, they are careful not to be seen. Now, if you'll excuse me, I need to clean up the remnants of my dinner."

Effectively dismissed.

Ignoring the sharp looks from Weston, Cassidy approached Ball and held out her business card. “If you can think of anything that would help our investigation, please call. My personal cell number is on the card, along with the station. Thank you for your time.”

He took the card, his fingers brushing hers. A chill slithered up her spine at the cold look in his eyes. This man did not like the police. “I will.” He dropped her card on the coffeetable, then opened the front door.

“One more thing.” Colin stopped in the doorway. “Maureen Monroe’s attacker would not have wanted to be seen either, yet he was. Are you sure no one can back up your story? There’s also one thing that is bothering me…the college had no Russell Ball on their roster. Your name only appears on the clinic records. Why is that?”

A muscle jerked in Ball’s undamaged cheek. “Another unfortunate mistake made twenty-five years ago by a second-rate college. Good day, officers. I’m sure if you dig a little harder, you’ll find your missing answers. But not here.”

~

Well played, Detective MacKenzie. Draco closed the door behind them with a definitive click. He’d almost panicked to see Cassidy at his door, but held his wits rather well, he thought.

Her gaze had landed on his scar without any trace of revulsion. Not so with the FBI agent. He’d seen her disgust and attempts to divert her gaze anywhere but at him. Perhaps the lovely agent would like to meet The Dragon in all his splendor.

They acted as if Maureen was the victim. Not so! He caressed his scar. He was the one left disfigured, his life ruined.

He opened his coat closet and ran his hands over the leather jacket with the embroidered dragon. All his followers would receive the same jacket once they'd proven themselves. Unfortunately, it wasn't happening as quickly as he'd like. Mary was very close, though.

At first, her work had been sloppy. Her last kill had shown a patience and finesse that gave Draco pleasure. He'd taught her well. Perhaps it was time to reward her. He picked up the phone from the end table and punched in her number.

He would wear his jacket when he killed the agent. Mary would wear hers on her next assignment. It was time for the world to become better acquainted with The Dragon and his minions.

~

Colin grabbed Cassidy's hand for a quick squeeze before she could pull away. "Don't worry. We'll catch the killer."

She slipped her hand free. "You keep saying that, and we keep coming up against dead ends."

"Faith, my dear." He held the back door open for her.

Rosie bounded out and lunged against the glass doors of the apartment complex.

"Rosie!" Cassidy dashed after her. She grabbed the dog's collar and glanced up.

On the other side of the glass, fear etched across his face, was Russell Ball. Draped over his arm was a leather jacket. She got a glimpse of a multi-colored design, but couldn't make out what it was.

"I'm sorry!" Cassidy tossed him a wave and dragged the barking dog back to the SUV. "What has gotten into you?" She glanced back to see Ball scurry into a parking garage. She'd be lucky if he didn't press charges over her brute of a dog.

"What's wrong?" Colin helped her get the struggling animal into the vehicle.

"I don't know. She's never acted like this before."

He stared in the direction of the parking garage. "They say dogs are good judges of character."

"Not so much." Cassidy climbed in and smiled. "She likes you, doesn't she?"

"Very funny." He closed the door and got into the front passenger seat.

"To the bar?" Weston asked.

"Onward, chauffeur." Colin clicked his seatbelt.

Cassidy laughed at the woman's uptight expression. She really needed to learn how to relax. If not, this case would kill them all.

~

Colin stared out the window and watched the trees pass. The dog's reaction to Ball stirred something in his gut. Could she be reacting to the man's fear or something else entirely? Maybe he wasn't her target. He tried to remember seeing someone else close by and drew a blank.

"What's going on in that pretty head of yours?" Weston asked.

"Did you see anyone else around when the dog went berserk?"

"A doorman, I think."

"What did he look like?"

"I couldn't see his face. Not past Ball, anyway. I noted the fancy red jacket and got in the car." She cut him a sideways glance. "Do I need to turn around?"

"Did you see the doorman when we went into the building?"

She shook her head and squealed tires turning the SUV back in the direction they'd come. "He's probably gone, but maybe someone can give us a description."

She drove right up to the doors and parked. "Monroe, stay with your dog. We don't need a repeat."

Colin sent Cassidy an apologetic look and jogged after Weston. They barged into the lobby of the complex. No doorman in sight.

"Excuse me." He approached a young man at a vending machine. "Does this place have a doorman or a security guard?"

"We have a guard, why? No fancy doorman, though."

"Does the guard wear red?"

The kid laughed. "Seriously? Have you ever seen one wear anything but blue or black?" The only one we have wearing red around here is crazy old lady Ethel. She wears a red cape with yellow fur every day, no matter what temperature it is. A real kook that one."

"Do you know where we can find her?"

"Nah. She leaves every day and comes back at odd times."

Colin clinched his fists. Another waste of time. Still, they needed to follow every lead.

"I'm sorry," Weston said as they returned to the SUV. "I'm originally from New York. We have doormen."

He exhaled sharply. "Did you see anyone out here, Cassidy?"

"Nope. Just me, Rosie, and the birds." She kicked the back of his seat. "Don't leave me again. I'm just as capable at investigating as either one of you and a whole lot safer with you than alone."

"Again, my apologies." Weston headed them back to the highway and to the bar as dusk descended over the trees.

A pink and green neon sign flashed Bar and Grill in twelve foot letters above the building. Colin hadn't stepped foot in a bar in several years. Not after having frequented one far more than was healthy after the shooting. He took a deep breath and shoved open the door to the SUV.

Flanked by Cassidy and Weston, he entered the bar and paused to allow his eyes to adjust to the dim light inside. The place was packed and several conversations halted as heads turned to study the newcomers. While some of the men might take it upon themselves to approach the beautiful women at Colin's side, anyone looking hard enough would be able to tell by their no-nonsense demeanor that they weren't there for a good time.

"I hate these meat markets." Cassidy marched to the bar and pulled a picture of their latest victim from her pocket. "Have you seen this woman?"

"Who's asking?" The bartender kept wiping the bar, not even glancing at the picture. The flamingo-style pink neon light behind him highlighted his bald head.

"FBI." Weston flashéd her badge.

"In that case." He glanced at the photo. "Yeah. A real looker. She was in here the other night."

"Alone?" Cassidy asked.

"It started out that way, then some man approached her. I could tell she didn't want anything to do with him, but she was polite. He bought her a glass of wine." He tapped his temple with his forefinger. "I remember all the beautiful ladies."

"What did the man look like?" Colin leaned against the bar, directing half his attention to the bartender and the other half at those watching them.

"A real ugly dude. Massive scar on his face. He came in with a plain Jane. She took a seat at the opposite end of the bar, and he approached our beauty. What did Miss Lovely do?"

"She was murdered."

The bartender blanched. "Seriously? Wow. Let me think a minute." He wiped his sweating scalp with the same rag he'd wiped the bar. "Yeah. She went to the restroom. I was helping another customer, but when I looked up, all three of them were gone.

"Is there a backdoor to this place?"

He pointed them to a sign that stated restrooms.

Cassidy went into the women's room, Weston studied the short hallway, and Colin shoved open the backdoor. No alarm sounded despite the warning sign on the wall. He glanced around, spotting a security camera. He'd bet the thing was disabled, too. Still, he called back to Weston to check on video footage before stepping onto the gravel paved alley behind the bar.

Several different tire tracks marred the gravel. Still, if they could get one to match the tread from the one they'd picked up at the crime scenes, they'd have proof the killer had stalked Megan Goodall, and murdered Lacey Goodall before that.

He pulled out his cellphone and placed a call to the office asking someone to tell him whether the two women were related. Turned out they're sisters. Interesting.

Now, all he needed to do was find out who would want to kill the sisters. He made a mental note to dig into their family history.

16

Back at Cassidy's house, Colin headed straight for the living room and his laptop. While he worked, the aroma of brewing coffee filled the place. Good. He'd be up late trying to make sense of all the pieces.

Cassidy set his mug on the coffee table next to his laptop. "Let's talk about it."

His head snapped up. "Now?" She couldn't be serious. Now was not the time to discuss what had almost happened between them.

"Why not?" She sat in an easy chair across from him and propped her feet on the coffee table. "We need to connect the dots."

"Wait. You're talking about the case?"

She frowned. "What else would I be talking about?"

"Nothing." Relief washed over him like a warm summer rain. "Let me check one more...yes. The Goodall sisters have a half sister. A Mary Jones." He pulled up her picture and turned the computer so

Cassidy could see the woman's photo. "Does she look like a Plain Jane to you?"

"The Dragon's accomplice?" She peered at the screen.

"Maybe." He jotted down her address. "You're a woman. How would you feel if your father married a woman then had two beautiful daughters."

"Sort of like Cinderella."

"What?"

"It's like the fairy tale, only The Dragon might be Mary's Prince Charming." She sipped her coffee. "Still, I'm not the type to get jealous over looks. I'm not a good person to ask."

"Pretend."

She stared over his head. "If I thought myself ugly, and scarred, I suppose I'd be jealous. Especially if a father that once lavished attention on me no longer had me at the center of his universe. But to kill someone? That's a stretch."

"If she's a follower of The Dragon, she might have the same outlook on pretty people that he does." Colin reached for his mug. "Maybe her half sisters were mean to her. Taunted her. Made fun of her."

Cassidy shrugged. "Let's assume she's deranged enough to go there. Other people have murdered after being bullied. We add her to our suspect list. Along with Russell Ball and our other scarred friends. Who else?"

"That's about it. We have tire tracks, fingerprints with no match in the system, and words drawn in the dirt." He ran his free hand through his hair. "I've never seen anything like it. I have a feeling the perp is right under our nose but we can't see him."

"What else do we know about Jones?" She reached down and rubbed Rosie's ears.

"She works as customer service at a department store. Turns out she doesn't have a medical background at all." He glanced at his monitor. "Lives on the outskirts of town in a trailer park. She lives a pretty unassuming life. Easily overlooked." Unlike the gorgeous woman wearing sweatpants and a loose tee shirt sitting across from him. Even in the most unsexy attire, he couldn't help but notice the heads turn when she'd entered the bar.

"You're staring." She raised her eyebrows.

"Sorry." He ducked his head. Careful man. *You're wearing your heart on your sleeve and she's made it more than clear what she thinks of a relationship with you*. His head agreed. Partners should never cross the line, but his heart had something else in mind. "First thing in the morning, we go visit Mary Jones."

She nodded, still absently scratching the dog's head. "Why do you suppose Rosie went berserk today?"

"Instinct? She saw someone we didn't or sensed something we missed?" Her behavior had nagged at him all day. So had the fear on Ball's face. "We need to take a closer look at Russell Ball. It bothers me that he isn't listed on the college roster. We need to find out what his name was before he changed it." He sent an email to Ingram. "I also want to talk to his neighbors.

Someone might know something they don't know they know."

"He's your number one?"

"Yep." He settled back on the sofa. His cell phone vibrated the same time Cassidy's beeped. He glanced at the text. "Help."

Cassidy jumped to her feet. "Mine says the same thing. It's Weston's number."

Their phones rang. Colin answered. "MacKenzie."

"Agent Ingram. I got a text from Weston. Isn't she with you?"

"She dropped us off an hour ago."

Ingram cursed. "Get to the motel. Now."

~

"Agent Weston?" Draco grinned when she opened the door to her motel room. "I have some information on the killer that is ravaging Clear Springs."

"How did you know where I was staying?" She peered past him into the parking lot.

He pushed his way inside, holding a Tazor to her ribcage. She jerked and fell like a board. "Why, I followed you, pretty one. You really should be more careful."

Her blue eyes blinked up at him. Words gurgled in her throat.

"You FBI agents think you're so smart, so above the rest of us." He grabbed her under the arms and dragged her to the bathroom.

He rolled her into the tub and tazed her again. No sense in letting Miss Beauty have the upper hand. He turned and tied her hands to the shower head, stretching her arms to an uncomfortable position. He then dug in her pockets, pulled out her cell phone, and sent a group text to all important contacts on her list.

"I really wish I had more time to play." He sat on the closed toilet. "You really are quite lovely."

"Why?"

"Why you?" He turned the damaged side of his face to her. "I saw the revulsion in your eyes earlier. You're no better than the other women I killed. Stay there. I'll be right back."

He dashed to his car, donned his leather jacket, then hurried back inside. He set up his video camera on the bathroom sink and pressed record. "We don't have much time." He pulled a knife from his pocket, careful to keep his face averted from the camera. "But, I can't disappoint the others, can I? They'll be expecting a video. I guess we have three or four minutes before I need to disappear." He shoved a washcloth in her mouth.

Using the knife, he popped the buttons from the white blouse she wore, revealing creamy skin. He softly drew the blade over her, counting her ribs as she screamed against her gag. Each scream sent his heart soaring! He closed his eyes and inhaled her fear.

After he'd had his fun, he put a bullet between her beautiful eyes and left, crushing her cell phone under his boot.

~

They made the fifteen minute drive in seven. Cassidy cut the jeep's engine and sprinted for the lobby, mere steps behind Colin. With one hand wrapped in Rosie's leash, she barged inside.

Ingram and Smith, their faces grave, turned from the counter to face them. "I want her found before I watch her death on camera," Ingram said. "I've tried her cell phone several times. Straight to voice mail. She doesn't answer a knock on the door of her room. Follow me." He grabbed a key from the shocked manager's hand and led the way.

"Find something," he barked, unlocking Weston's room door.

"What's her name, sir?" Cassidy withdrew her weapon. "We only know her as Weston."

"Maggie." He choked on her name.

They stepped into a ransacked room. The quilt from the bed lay half on the floor. A chair lay on its side. "Maggie Weston?" Cassidy moved toward the bathroom.

She froze. Maggie lay in the tub, a bullet hole in the center of her forehead and thin cuts across her ribcage. Written on the mirror in what looked like blood were the words, 'The pretty must die'.

"In here." Cassidy stepped over a shattered cell phone.

Ingram joined her and groaned. "Maggie." He knelt next to her body. "Why you?"

"No offense, sir," Cassidy said, sliding her gun into her holster, "but she fits the profile. She's quite beautiful." She turned to Colin. "For her to be targeted, she had to have met her killer and been repulsed by him, or at least he thought she had been."

"Russell Ball."

She nodded. "He's the only one we know of that she questioned for any length of time."

Ingram glanced up with red-rimmed eyes. "I want that bastard hung by his testicles."

"We're trying, sir. We don't have any solid evidence against him." Cassidy backed from the bathroom as emergency responders arrived.

"Find some! Get him behind bars. And, Monroe...get out of those sweats. We want this guy coming to us."

He had come to them and look what happened. She glanced at Colin as fear slithered up her back and wrapped its tentacles around her throat. "He's better than me, than us. We can't catch him. He's like a ghost." She'd known all along she didn't have what it took to be a good detective. This proved it.

Colin placed a hand on each of her shoulders and shook her. "Stop it. You will catch this guy. You're a great detective. One of the best I've ever worked with."

"How do you do that? How do you always seem to know what I'm thinking?" She locked gazes with him as if turning away would cause her to lose her grip on reality. "I don't think I can draw him out. He knows where I am. He can come get me any time he wants. He doesn't want to. He's toying with me." How could he? Especially if he was her biological father as they suspected? Who treated their child this way? If The Dragon wanted her, he could have her.

"Let's head to his apartment. If he's gone, I want to call a press conference." She pulled away from Colin. "We'll give out his description and name. Somebody out there has seen him and knows where he is."

"That's my girl."

They headed to Ball's apartment. Cassidy wasn't surprised in the slightest to find him gone. The manager let them into his apartment, a place Cassidy doubted he would return to.

With Colin starting at one end, and her at the other, they made a slow sweep of the place and came up with nothing. No photos, no books, nothing personal in any way. It was if the man had never been there.

"Who are you?"

Cassidy turned to see an elderly woman in a bright red coat with a fur collar died a sunshine yellow. Weston's doorman? "I'm Detective Monroe, this is Detective MacKenzie. Do you know the man who lived here?"

"No one lived here, dear. Well, there was a poor soul who came in and out, but he never slept here."

"Did he have a scar?"

"Oh, yes, the poor thing. I've often wondered how that came to be. That man has a story to tell, mark my words." Without actually entering the apartment, she poked her head in and looked around. "Very clean."

"When was the last time you saw Mr. Ball?" Cassidy took her by the arm and drew her into the hall.

"Why..." she plucked at a stray hair on her chin. "Less than an hour ago, I'd say. He told me goodbye as we passed in the hall. It sounded pretty final. What am I supposed to do with all his newspapers?"

"Newspapers?" Cassidy peered into her face.

"Why yes. He was always placing ads and said he kept them for prosperity's sake. Since he came and went so often and hired a cleaning crew for the apartment, he asked me to hold on to them. Shall I give them to you?" She clapped a white-gloved hand over her mouth. "Is he dead? Did he have an accident? Oh, dear."

"No, ma'am. He's fine. The newspapers?"

"Oh, yes. Right this way." She unlocked a door across the hall.

Cassidy was immediately assaulted by the odor of several cats. Breathing as shallowly as possible, she followed the strange woman into the apartment. Next to a rickety kitchen table were several newspapers.

"See? The man was always placing ads. I couldn't find out which ones, though," the woman said. "He didn't sign his name."

Cassidy knew which ones would be his. "What was he wearing when you last saw him?"

"A leather jacket with a dragon stitched on the back. Quite fetching. He carried more of the same jackets in his arms."

17

Cassidy woke early the next morning, made a pot of coffee, poured herself a cup, and then headed to the basement. Something had been teasing at the corner of her mind. She'd missed something that would, without a doubt, point to Russell Ball as her mother's attacker. Time would tell whether he was also the one who had murdered her, although her suspicions ran strong that he was. There couldn't be two evil masterminds out there who left the message 'the pretty must die' next to his victims.

She dug back through her mother's things and pulled out a shoebox full of photos. She'd seen some from her mother's college days and hadn't thought much of them...until that morning.

One after another the photos were set aside until she came across the one haunting her. She peered at the young man with his arm around her mother's shoulders. Russell Ball, handsome, grinning, and scarless. Mom had known her attacker. No wonder she'd gone away from the party with him.

"What are you doing?" Colin came down the steps. "I got worried when I didn't see you on the sofa."

"Look." She handed him the picture. "I think they might have dated. They at least knew each other."

His eyes lit up as a grin spread across his face. "This is a great find."

She glanced away before doing something she'd regret, like throwing her arms around his neck in celebration. Instead, she petted Rosie, craving physical contact with a breathing being. "All we have to do now is find him."

"And Mary Jones." He sat on the bottom step. "This case is coming to a close. Can you feel it?"

She felt a lot of things, one of which was the tender feeling she got when he slept and she could watch him without getting caught. She'd heard him cry out again last night, but had done no more than peek into his room. What she'd wanted to do was lie beside him and comfort him.

"I hope so," she said. "I've never been challenged this way before. It's...unsettling the way the body count is adding up."

He held out his hand. "Come. Let's have breakfast and then visit Mary Jones."

Her gaze clashed with his as she put her hand in his larger one. Heat infused her. The moment she was on her feet, she pulled free. Close contact with Colin only muddled her mind.

That morning, he'd cooked pancakes and sausage. At this rate, Cassidy would have no other choice than to wear her sweats.

After eating, she donned her suit, clipped her hair back from her face and applied a smattering of makeup. A lot of bother to hunt down criminals. Still, Ingram had ordered her, and with him grieving the loss of Weston, she'd do as he wanted.

"I do like you in a suit," Colin said, handing her Rosie with her leash attached. "Gorgeous."

Her face heated. "Thanks." This type of attention was why she dressed in clothes suited for cleaning out the garage. She didn't welcome the attention. Beauty got her mother killed. Why advertise the fact she'd inherited her mother's looks?

"I know what you're thinking."

"Oh, yeah?" She slid into the front passenger seat, surprised at how easy she gave over control of the driving to Colin.

"You think beauty is something to shove aside, hide under the rug." He started the ignition. "It won't work. Your beauty shines through even in sweats. Embrace what God gave you. It's a gift."

She supposed he accepted his good looks with open arms. She'd seen him use his manly assets to distract witnesses upon finding a dead body. Even Weston had faltered in her chilly attitude a time or two when he poured on the charm.

"What do you think about Ball fleeing his apartment with an armload of matching jackets?" She cut Colin a sideways glance.

"I think we need to be vigilant and worried. It sounds like he's outfitting a small army."

That's what she thought, too, and the idea sent dread flooding through her. How many followers did he have? Even a few could leave a path of destruction worse than Clear Springs, or even the state of Arkansas, had ever seen. She clicked her seatbelt. They'd already seen more death than she'd ever thought to experience on the job in a small southern town.

While Colin drove, she called Ingram to check in and give him their plan for the morning. "We're headed to the last known address of Mary Jones."

"You shouldn't go without backup."

"You're welcome to meet us there, sir, but every angle needs to be explored immediately. We also found a photo of my mother at the college frat party with Russell Ball. I don't think that was his name back then."

"I'll have someone check on that. If he changed his name legally, there'll be records. Be careful." Click.

He'd no sooner hung up than her phone rang again. "Detective Monroe here."

"Detective this is Mr. Laraby, from the college. Do you remember me?"

"Yes, sir, I remember you."

"You said to call if I discovered anything. Well, I remember something."

She heard the rustling of papers.

"Your mother's roommate here was Allison Bergeron. Since I didn't have her as a student, her name skipped my mind until I started going through school rosters."

"Why would you be doing that, sir?" She glanced at Colin.

"Something about that night was bothering me. Not just the violence of your mother's attack, but that no one did anything about it afterward. Those boys dropped her off at the clinic and left the party."

"We have a photo of my mother with the man we believe attacked her. Do you think you could identify him?"

"Maybe. If he was one of my students. I'm here until noon if you want to stop by."

"Thank you." She hung up. "Detour," she told Colin. "Head back to the college." She called Ingram back and gave him Bergeron's name. "Call me when you have an address."

"Will do." Click.

The man was short on words that morning. She sighed. The death of someone who meant a lot to you did that.

~

Colin parked in front of the cafeteria and walked next to Cassidy and Rosie. Mr. Laraby sat at the same table as the last time they'd spoken to him.

The man looked up with a grim smile. "I'm sorry for having you drive all the way back out here."

"If it helps us solve the case, it was time worth spent." Colin pulled out a chair for Cassidy then took one to the man's right.

"This is the picture." Cassidy handed the photo to Laraby.

"Yes, I know this man." Laraby leaned back in his chair. "Smart. A real ladies man, back in the day. His name is Blake Russell."

Colin exchanged a glance with Cassidy. "You're sure? He registered here under that name?"

"Yes, but he wasn't enrolled here at the time of the attack. He received his bachelor's in business early. I always figured he would be a very wealthy man someday."

"Would that have kept him from being invited to the party?" Colin rested his folded arms on the table.

"Not at all. Not with his popularity."

Hmm. Being a handsome, sought after young man, the disfigurement to his face could easily have sent him into a psychotic rage. He could have harbored a grudge for years until deciding to kill Maureen. All they had to do now was find out where he was hiding.

Cassidy checked her phone. "We have an address for Allison."

"You've been a big help, Mr. Laraby." Colin stood and shook the man's hand. "Please call if you think of anything else."

"I will. Good luck."

Colin and Cassidy hurried back to the jeep. "I still think we need to check Mary's address before questioning Allison," he said.

"I agree. A killer in one hand is worth a potential witness from twenty-five years ago in the other."

They sped back toward Clear Springs and the rundown trailer park at the edge of town. Colin drove slowly through the mobile homes until he spotted Mary's address. He passed the rusty trailer and parked a few homes down.

"If you're looking for weird Mary, she ain't home." A toothless old woman in the mobile home next to Mary's blew a plume of smoke into the air. "Packed up her Ford and skedaddled this morning before sunup."

"Are you sure she left?" Colin stopped and faced her.

"Had a couple of suitcases. That's good enough for me."

If they hadn't had breakfast...no, missing Mary was just one more broken link in the chain. One more thing that kept The Dragon and his minions one step ahead of the authorities.

He thanked the woman and continued to Mary's trailer. They might find something. No stone could be left unturned.

The door to Mary's trailer hung open by a couple of inches. Withdrawing his weapon, Colin motioned for Cassidy to stay behind him.

"Send Rosie in first." She unhooked the leash from the dog's collar. "She'll alert us if anyone is inside. Search, Rosie."

When minutes passed and no warning bark came from inside, Colin entered the trailer, wrinkling his nose at the sour odor of spoiled food and the mustiness of mounds of newspapers and magazines. "What a mess."

"It figures she'd be a hoarder. A lot of hurting people are. We'll be in here forever searching through all…this." Cassidy waved an arm at mounds of clutter that barely left enough room for a person to walk.

"We'll start by looking for something that seems out of place or of significance." He reholstered his gun and headed down the short hallway to a bedroom.

Rosie nosed in a closet and gave a short wuff when Colin approached.

"Back, girl."

Colin squatted and shoved aside a mound of clothes to reveal a calico cat and five kittens. He glanced around for a basket or box of some kind, finally emptying a clothes basket and moving mama and babies inside. He carried the basket back to the front room and set it on the crowded kitchen table where Cassidy flipped through a small pile of newspapers.

"We've been looking through larger editions. What if there's something important in these smaller presses? What's that? Oh." She picked up one of the kittens, nuzzling it against her cheek. "You poor little thing."

"I guess we'll be making a stop at the pound." Colin sat and pulled several of the papers to his side of the table.

She placed the kitten back with its mother and opened another newspaper to the classifieds. A few minutes later, she gasped. "I know how he's getting his followers." She shoved the paper at Colin.

Circled in red was an advertisement that read:

Mistreated?
Pretty people treating you unfairly?
Has your life been forever changed because of THEIR treatment?
Call 555-212-3456
I can help if you're willing to do the work

18

After calling in and securing the crime scene at Mary Jones's trailer, Cassidy and Colin drove toward the address they had for Allison Bergeron. Strange how so few people moved out of the area after college. Perhaps, they'd gone, realized life wasn't greener outside of Arkansas, and moved back.

"I spent my childhood convincing myself that my father was some kind of hero killed while saving people. Maybe a fireman or the military. Mom never talked about him, so I built up this fantasy. Wow, was I wrong." Cassidy took a shuddering sigh. "I couldn't have been further from the truth." An ache took up residence deep in her heart. Not only was she the product of rape, but she was the child of a serial killer.

Colin took her hand. "We can't help where we come from. We only have control over where we're going."

"You're wise for such a pretty face." She tried to smile, and failed. How would she react when facing her father for the last time? Could she pull the trigger? If she'd known Russell Ball was the man who'd fathered her and killed her mother, she would have shot him where he stood. Yes, she'd be able to pull the trigger.

"Let's grab some coffee." Colin swerved the jeep into a drive thru coffee shop. "You need something to bolster your spirits."

She glanced at him, studying the strong jaw line, the etched lips, the concern in his eyes. "Kiss me."

A crooked smile spread across his face. "Needing a distraction?"

"I know it's not professional, and I told you to keep your—"

He cupped the back of her head and kissed her long and hard until she could think of nothing but breathing. When they were both gasping, he drew back. "Did it work?"

"Thank you." She chuckled. "You're good medicine, Colin MacKenzie. I'm sorry about what I said the other night, you know, about being your pain killer."

He squeezed her hand. "Let's help each other through this, then we'll have time to explore us." He released her and pulled up to the window. "You can use me for whatever you need to in the meantime."

"Excuse me?" The barrista at the window widened her eyes.

"Sorry." Colin laughed and placed their orders.

Soon, they were back on the road, still chuckling over the expression on the poor barrista's face. "I think you disappointed her," Cassidy said. "She would have loved to be your plaything, I think."

"She was cute, but I prefer a more mature woman." He winked.

Was there a future for them? Cassidy stared out the window at the thick trees zooming past on the sides of the highway. She'd never really considered a man in her life. Her career, proving herself, those had always taken precedence. Dare she hope for something more?

What kind of man wanted a woman with her blood line? If she'd thought proving herself in a predominantly male career in the south was hard before, once people found out who her father was, it could become near to impossible. She could move. Start fresh somewhere else. It was a thought.

They parked in front of a modest ranch-style home in a neighborhood of cookie cutter houses. On the front porch sat assorted shoes in varying sizes. A tricycle lay on its side on the freshly mowed lawn. A porch swing moved by a gentle breeze. A scene of tranquility. One which Colin and Cassidy were about to disrupt.

"Let's go meet your mother's bestfriend." Colin shoved open his door.

Cassidy's heart went into overdrive. They were about to speak with the woman who had known her mother better than anyone. She squared her shoulders, commanded Rosie to stay, and marched to the front door. On second thought, she snapped her fingers for Rosie to follow. They might be in the house for a while and the day was heating up. If Allison didn't want a dog in the house, Rosie could stay on the porch.

The door opened before Cassidy's finger pressed the bell. A pretty woman with a stylish blond bob haircut answered the door. "Baby is sleeping." She smiled. "I hope you aren't selling anything."

Cassidy showed her badge. "We have a few questions for you. Are you Allison Bergeron?"

The woman's brows drew together in a frown. "Not anymore. I haven't been her in twenty years. I'm Allison Carson now. What's this about?"

"May we come in or would you prefer the porch?" Cassidy glanced at a set of whicker rocking chairs.

"Come in." She eyed the dog, then her gaze rested appreciatively on Colin. "The dog won't make noise will it? I have a three year old inside that would love to play with it."

"She's well trained," Cassidy said, drawing the woman's attention back to her.

Allison opened the door wide and allowed them to enter. "Can I get you something to drink?"

"We've coffee, thank you." Colin smiled, putting the woman at ease.

How did he do that with a look and a grin? Cassidy shook her head and sat on one end of the sofa. "We were told by a Mr. Wilson that you were Maureen Monroe's bestfriend in college."

"Yes." Allison sat in a stuffed chair covered with a floral fabric. "Benji, play nice with the dog."

"Gentle, Rosie." Cassidy watched as a tow-headed little boy squatted next to the dog.

“I haven’t seen or heard from Maureen in…at least ten years. We used to keep in touch, then nothing.”

Cassidy took a deep breath. “She was murdered ten years ago. We believe by the same man who attacked her during the frat party.”

“Oh.” Tears sprang to Allison’s eyes and she glanced at her son. “Benji, go get a juice box out of the fridge, okay?” Once he’d gone, Rosie trotting at his side, she turned back to Cassidy. “He’ll probably give your dog cookies, I hope that’s okay.” She sighed. “I had no idea Maureen was dead. And…that awful night.” She covered her face with her hands. “I’ve done everything possible to forget that night.”

She hadn’t wanted to go to the party. I coerced her. It was all my fault. If she hadn’t been there…”

“If I know my mother, she had a mind of her own.”

“You’re her daughter? Of course you are. I can see the resemblance.” She reached over and placed a hand on Cassidy’s arm. “You’re just as pretty as she…was.”

“Can you tell me about her?”

“A great gal. Oh, the fun we had. I was the troublemaker, Maureen the logical one. Still, she had her wild side. She went to the party because a boy she thought was handsome was going.”

“Blake Russell?”

“Yes, that’s the one. Your mother wasn’t a prude, but she was one of the good girls. That’s why her attack affected so many of us the way it did. I was promiscuous. It should have been me in the woods that night.” Tears trickled down her face. “I’ve never forgiven myself. If I hadn't been with my own boy that night...well, things can't be changed, can they?"

"No, ma'am." A knife stabbed at Cassidy's gut. "If only they could. We have reason to believe that Blake was her attacker that night and the one who later killed her. We also believe he is responsible for the deaths of a couple of other women."

"Oh, no." Her sobs increased.

Colin knelt next to the woman's chair. "None of it is your fault, Allison. You can't force someone to do something they don't want to. Things got carried away at that party, things that resulted in future destruction. You weren't at fault. We're not here to make you feel bad. We're hoping you can give us some answers. Maybe tell us more about Blake Russell."

"He was a handsome enigma. Smart, finished college early. All the girls wanted to be noticed by him, but he only had eyes for Maureen. Called her his Fire Princess. I would never have figured him for a killer."

"My mother wounded him that night." Cassidy stared at the freshly vacuumed carpet. "Gravely wounded him. We think that is what set him on his path of destruction."

Rosie barked from the kitchen.

Cassidy lunged to her feet at the same moment Colin did. They dashed into the kitchen.

Rosie lunged at the kitchen door, keeping her body between the door and the child. The twisted features of Blake Russell stared through the window, then vanished.

Colin unlocked then yanked open the door. "Give the command, Cassidy."

"Angriff!"

Rosie darted outside, Colin and Cassidy on her heels. They chased her around the corner of the house.

Blake grabbed for the door of a dark sedan left running. With his other hand, he tazed the dog, then slid into the driver's seat. He squealed tires backing from the driveway.

Colin knelt and fired off two shots while Cassidy called Ingram and knelt beside the helpless Rosie.

The shots shattered the back window of the sedan and Cassidy watched helplessly as Russell sped away. "Good girl." Once Rosie was back on her feet, albeit a bit wobbly, Cassidy turned and headed for the kitchen.

Allison clutched her son to her chest while a baby screamed from a room on the other side of the house. "Thank God I keep that door locked. Was that Blake?"

"Yes." Cassidy glanced out the front window. He'd followed them. "We'll need to put your family in protective custody."

~

Oh, the game was getting fun now! Draco grinned as he sped away from the blond woman's house. He remembered her from college. Pretty, but in no way close to Maureen's beauty. He wanted to go back after the cops left and show her who he was now, but the innocence in the little boy's eyes wouldn't allow him to.

He didn't harm children. They weren't responsible for any revulsion they might show. If they cried when seeing him, he blamed the parents for not raising them better. He caressed his scar. He'd always wanted a son. Instead, he had a daughter, beautiful like her mother, who hunted him like an animal.

Someday, when the time was right, they'd face each other in a final, epic battle. The strongest would survive. He had no qualms that they would ever be a loving family. He was meant to be alone. The last of a dying breed. The lone dragon on a quest to rid the world of the unworthy.

He popped Beethoven's Fifth into the CD player and drummed his hands on the steering wheel in beat with the music. The next few weeks would be glorious as he continued his diabolical game. He laughed, the sound ringing loud over the music.

Sweet Cassidy, can you hear the music? He'd make sure it was the last thing she ever heard, his face the last thing she saw. Just like Maureen.

19

Mary Jones checked into a motel in the next town and cursed The Dragon. She immediately repented. She couldn't stay mad at the man who gave her back her purpose in life.

She tossed her suitcases in the corner and threw herself across the bed. How had the cops found out about her? Draco had promised there was no way to be discovered. It had to be because of her hateful sisters. They were at the root of all her problems.

Well, no more. She laughed, the sound manic in the small room. They couldn't create problems for anyone anymore.

She glanced at the water-stained ceiling. What did she do now? She had no others on her list. Most people were kind, if not sympathetic to Mary's plainness. It wasn't her fault she had mousy hair and mud-colored eyes. Nor was it her fault she'd struggled with being overweight her entire life. Her mother had been attractive, her father handsome. It was nothing more than the luck of the draw.

Sighing, she pounded the mattress and dug her cell phone out of her purse. "What do I do now?" she asked the moment he answered. "I have no other purpose."

"Find one." Draco's deep voice resonated over the air waves. "But we don't kill those who don't deserve it. You must remember that. Find a new identity for yourself. All the information you need is in the packet I gave you at the first meeting. Our time of working together is complete."

"No." Her heart beat in her throat. "I want to continue helping you. Tell me what to do. Please."

"Find your purpose again, Mary." Click.

She grinned, knowing exactly what she would do. Something that would make her Draco's favorite.

~

Rosie seemed to suffer no ill effects from being tazed, much to Cassidy's relief. She sat on the porch of Allison's house, her arm around the dog, and waited while Ingram and the crime scene investigators prepared her and her family to be moved.

A navy Toyota Camry pulled into the driveway. A harried man shoved open his door and, leaving it hanging open, bounded up the porch steps, not sparing Cassidy a glance. Mr. Carson, she presumed.

Colin met the man at the door, saying something to him in a low, soothing voice. Her partner would be a wonder in hostage negotiations. He had a way about him that put the most anxious person at ease. Except for her. The deep rumble of his voice sent her senses into overdrive instead of soothing them.

Since The Dragon seemed to be mirroring Cassidy's steps, Ingram had asked her and Colin to take the Carsons to the safe house and leave the rest of the investigation to the FBI. The order raised the hackles on the back of her neck. This was her case! It was personal. The last thing she wanted was to be hidden away in some mountain cabin with a guard watching her every move.

"But, my job. Our life," Mr. Carson argued. "We can't leave it. This killer isn't after us or he would have harmed my wife and son."

"Sir, it's only until he's caught. It's a precaution. Think of your family."

Cassidy turned her head as Colin placed a consoling hand on the man's shoulder. She pushed to her feet. "The killer wants me, Mr. Carson. Rest assured we'll do everything in our power to keep us all safe."

He narrowed his eyes. "Yet, you're the officer going with us, right?"

"Yes, sir, I've been ordered to hide the same as you." She motioned for Rosie to follow and pushed into the house. She approached Ingram. "I'd like permission to go to my home and pack a few things."

"Smith and MacKenzie, take Monroe to her place. Be back in an hour. We're wasting daylight." He gave Cassidy a nod and marched to the kitchen where Allison packed a box with food. "Ma'am we only have so much room in the jeep."

"My babies have to eat."

Cassidy smiled and joined her bodyguards outside. An hour later, a few changes of clothing, toiletries, her mother's journal and her case notes, and Cassidy sat in the idling jeep while FBI agents she had yet to meet loaded her vehicle with everything a family thought they couldn't live without. When the jeep was full, they loaded the family's silver mini-van. She shook her head. A lot of baggage to cart up the mountain.

"This is ridiculous," Colin said, getting into the driver's seat. "That woman doesn't want to leave anything behind."

"She wants her family comfortable." Which would be a lot more than she and Colin would be. The two bedroom safehouse left the two of them sleeping on the floor in the front room in much too close proximity to each other. Still, the family would provide a safe buffer between the tension radiating between her and her partner no matter how much they tried to pretend as if nothing was happening between them.

"It bothers me that Ingram is removing us from the case, so to speak." Colin backed out of the drive. "We were beginning to make headway."

"I agree. If one of us had to go into hiding, it should have been me, leaving you to continue the investigation."

"No way." He frowned. "Where you go, I go. It's been that way since day one." He took her hand. "I'd go crazy not knowing how you were or whether Blake was getting close."

His words warmed her to the bone. “I appreciate the thought, but I trust you to help me more than anyone else.”

He grinned. “I don’t intend to stop investigating completely. I’ll just be doing it through cyber space. Everyone leaves a trail. We just have to find Blake’s.”

“Don’t forget Mary.”

He chuckled. “How could I forget our crazy Plain Jane? No, I’ll be searching for her right along with her leader.”

“Why do you think none of his other followers have come forth? He has to have them. Why else have an armload of jackets? Do you think he’s working with them one-by-one? Other than Mary, we’ve only met the one posing as a photographer and nothing on him since.” Nothing about this case was easy. It was one for the history books. They could have saved so much time if her mother would have mentioned her attacker’s name in her journal.

Why hadn’t she? Why keep it a secret? Had her mother had a personal vendetta against Blake that led to a showdown she lost? So many questions, so few answers.

“What do you think about Ingram sending the Carsons to the safehouse?” she asked. “If Blake had wanted to harm them, he had the opportunity. At least with the little boy.”

“Allison is a good-looking woman. I don’t think Ingram wants to take any chances. Maybe Blake has a few morals and doesn’t harm children. But, if he wanted to go after their mother…well, you know what it's like to have your mother murdered."

She did. Her later teen years had been ones full of difficulty, pity, and rebellion. She wouldn't wish that on anyone. "I still don't like being sent away."

"We'll manage." He squeezed her hand and pulled free as he turned the jeep down a side road that didn't look as if anyone had driven there in a long time.

Weeds covered the dirt road, hiding the ruts. The jeep bounced over one hole after another until Cassidy thought her teeth would break from clacking together. She breathed a sigh of relief when they pulled in front of the rustic cabin. "Home sweet home for however long we're destined to stay." She opened her door, then Rosie's. "Check it out, girl."

The dog bounded away, nose to the ground as Cassidy turned to survey their surroundings. Thick trees and underbrush provided plenty of places for a person to hide. Someone should have kept the place up a bit more. It might prove to be more of a danger than a safe place.

She scanned the tree line. The sun barely cut through the thick branches overhead. Several trees hung low over the cedar roofed cabin. There'd be no fires until they were trimmed back. It was a good thing it was summer and not winter. "I'll head inside and open the windows to air the place out," she told Colin as the mini-van pulled behind the jeep.

She marched to the front door and pushed it open with a loud squeak. Two mice darted across the floor, leaving tracks in the thick dust on the floor. At least she'd keep busy cleaning.

Who was she kidding? She didn't want to clean. She wanted to hunt down and confront her murderous father.

20

Cassidy and Allison had the cabin liveable by nightfall. Then, boredom quickly set in. While Colin worked his magic on the internet, Cassidy set her mother's caseboard up in the cabin's dining space. She hoped that by taking everything down and putting everything back up, she'd discover something she might have previously missed.

"What is that?" Bill Carson stood next to her, arms crossed.

"A case board on a cold case related to the one we're working on now." She leaned against a small wooden table and stared at the board.

"These photos look old." He peered closer at the ones saved by Cassidy's mother. "Is the killer here?"

Cassidy pointed him out. "We have no idea where he is now."

"That's Blake Russell. I went to high school with him."

"What?!" She whirled, sloshing hot coffee on her hand. She hissed and wiped it on the leg of her jeans.

"Yeah. He comes from a rather influential family, at least for this area. A bit of a spoiled brat, smart, and athletic. Leader of the popular group. Last I heard, he'd made a bundle of money for himself in real estate."

She couldn't believe their luck. "You wouldn't happen to know the name of his company, would you? He's changed his name since you knew him. He goes by Russell Ball."

"Wyvern Incorporated."

Of course. Cassidy clapped him on the shoulder. "Thank you." Maybe being locked up with the Carsons wouldn't be so bad after all. She headed to the living room where Colin sat hunched over his laptop. "Look up Wyvern Incorporated. Bill said it's Blake's corporate name."

"Wyvern as in dragon? How dense could we be?"

"In our defense, I didn't expect him to be a wealthy owner of anything."

Colin's fingers flew over the keyboard. "The company was sold for five million dollars last year." He leaned back on the sofa. "Another dead end."

"No." She sagged next to him. "He planned this. He built up the business, sold it, and started creating havoc."

"He has the money to lay low for a while, too." He started typing again. A few minutes later, he groaned. "Most of his funds are in an off-shore account."

"Of course, they are." They were never going to catch him. Not usually given to self-pity, Cassidy blinked back tears. She'd been sad and cried at her mother's death, devastated for months, but these were tears of frustration and helplessness. Sometimes, when the day seemed darkest, she almost turned to the God her mother believed in.

Colin put his arms around her and pulled her close. "Please don't cry. Don't give up on me, sweetheart." His thick brogue smoothed the edges of her pain.

She rested her head on his shoulder and closed her eyes, suddenly exhausted. If only she could stay there. If only she were worthy of having a career and love. But, she wasn't. It took everything she had to do her job the way she thought it needed doing and in one fell swoop, Blake Russell took that all away. Now, even if she felt there was room in her life for romance, she couldn't foist her bloodline on anyone. Most of all any possible future children.

Squeezing her eyes tight, tears trickled down her cheeks. Enough pity. She swiped the tears away and sat up. "What's our next move?"

~

"We pass on any information we have to Ingram." Colin felt an immediate loss when she pulled away. At least she was no longer treating him as if he were going to attack her or give her some fatal disease. It seemed as if she's chosen to pass off their...misunderstanding and continue as friends, if not close partners. He'd take what he could get. There was plenty of time for more in the future. "At least we've gone a few days without another death." She pushed to her feet and spread a sleeping bag on the floor. "I'm bushed, Colin. I'm going to sleep."

He nodded. "I'll take first watch and wake you in four hours."

While she settled in the close area between the sofa and the wall, Rosie curled up next to her and the rest of the cabin's occupants headed to their prospective rooms. The Carson's youngest wailed in protest at going to bed but settled down within minutes. Soon, soft snores drifted from Cassidy's makeshift bed.

He shifted in his seat so he could see her in the light of the laptop monitor. Shadows flickered across her face. Long lashes rested on soft cheeks. Lips, begging to be kissed, parted slightly in sleep. Her beauty did things to him that no other woman had ever done. Not only her outward appearance, but the beauty within. Her strength and determination. Still, he saw her vulnerability and knew he'd die protecting her if it came to that.

A board creaked overhead. Bill Carson most likely paced the floor in his own attempts to protect his family. Moments later the man joined him downstairs.

"You should sleep, Mr. Carson." Colin closed his laptop to prevent the man from seeing confidential information.

"I can't. Not when there is a madman out there who might want to harm my wife." He ran his hands through his hair. "Agent Ingram let me bring my pistol. I haven't fired the thing in years."

"Can you shoot another person?" A lot of people couldn't.

"If it means them or my family, I won't hesitate." He pulled up one of the four straight-back kitchen chairs and swung it around, straddling it and resting his folded arms on the back. "I hope it doesn't come to violence."

"We'll do our best to keep it away from you." Colin glanced at Cassidy. "It's her he wants, not your wife. If he were to go after your wife, it would be to get to the detective."

"It upsets me to think the FBI would put my family in more danger by sending the detective with us." The corners of his mouth turned down.

"She's good at what she does. If we're wrong, and the unsub has targeted your wife for a reason known only to him, Detective Monroe is an asset you want on your side."

"I guess I'll have to take your word for it, won't I?"

Colin understood the man's anger. He felt his own. "You should get some sleep."

The man smiled. "I know a dismissal when I hear one. Good night, Detective." Bill replaced the chair and headed back up the stairs.

Colin watched him leave then opened up his laptop. He needed to find the one needle in the haystack that would give them the upper hand in a case quickly growing out of control.

"Don't blame him for being angry," Cassidy mumbled from the floor. "I'm angry, too. None of us asked for this."

He nudged her gently with his foot. "I don't. Go back to sleep. I'm sorry we woke you."

He eyed the backpack next to the front door. His prescription sleep aids were in there. While he hated to take one, he wondered whether having a nightmare in a houseful of strangers might be worse.

~

Mary backed down the rough dirt road and onto the highway. Cackling, she parked on the shoulder and dialed Draco. "I know where she's hiding," she said in a sing-song voice.

"I thought you were going to disappear and start over."

"I want to help you. Without you, I'm nothing." Why couldn't he see that? Start over? He'd given her a new life, a new purpose. Why would she want to be anywhere else?

Silence screamed from the other end of conversation.

"Draco?"

"When I give you a direct order, Mary, I expect you to follow it. Do not engage Detective Monroe. I will deal with her myself. Do you understand?"

"Yes, sir." She understood perfectly. He wanted something done with the detective and the fact she still walked the earth meant he didn't know what to do about her. Mary could read between the lines better than most people. She understood the need for secrecy. "I'll do as you say." Click.

She drummed her hands on the steering wheel in a beat of celebration. When she did what needed to be done, Draco would love her above all others.

~

Imbecile! She was going to ruin everything.

Draco leaned back in his leather chair. What to do about Mary? She was going to ruin everything.

He needed to give her a job to do. One that would get her captured, or better yet, killed. If that didn't work, he'd have to dispose of her himself. Poor Mary. He saw the look of longing in her eyes. She was so desperate for love she'd take even a disfigured man such as himself. Perhaps there really was someone for everyone in this world. If only she weren't so...annoying, and a little more attractive. He would never desire a pretty person again. Not after having discovered the ugliness inside them. Still, he wanted someone that he could stomach looking at over the table at mealtime. Perhaps, he was a bit of a hypocrite.

Pushing to his feet, he crossed the small amount of space in the cramped apartment and stared out the window at the mini-mart across the street. He could have rented a much nicer place, but a dump like this one would be the last place the authorities would suspect. Living in the seedy side of town had its benefits and after putting a bullet between the eyes of a young gang member without batting an eye, the locals left him alone.

Draco needed a distraction. He shoved his arms into the sleeves of his leather jacket and headed outside. Even he could buy companionship with the right amount of money. He had ten tons of stress bottled up inside of him and desperately needed a release.

He scoured the streets looking for a woman with a bit of class. So many of them were skanky or shied away when they saw him coming. Unfortunately, the shooting of the gang member had made so many of the women afraid of him.

Keeping the good side of his face to them, he approached a group where a young woman of about eighteen smiled shyly up at him. He didn't recognize her. While sweet, she wasn't beautiful in the typical sense and wore tight jeans and a shirt that didn't show every one of her assets. Just the type of girl to wile away a few hours.

"Are you eighteen, and can you stomach this for a hundred dollars?" He showed her his scar.

Her eyes widened. "As long as you don't do that to me, I can."

"I like your style, young lady." He crooked his arm. "Two hours company is all I desire. Do you prefer red or white wine?"

"Pink champagne." She batted her lashes.

He laughed. "Then pink champagne it shall be." He bowed to the other prostitutes. "She'll be back in a little while, safe and sound."

After stopping at a liquor store on the corner and keeping his face turned from security cameras, he purchased the best pink champagne the store carried and escorted his little friend back to his apartment.

"Have a seat, darling. There's a change of clothes on the table. What is your name?"

"What do you want my name to be?"

"Maureen." He grinned. "You wouldn't happen to have red hair under that black wig, would you?"

She giggled and yanked off the wig. Strawberry blond curls tumbled to her shoulders.

It might not be the same shade as the woman he'd once idolized, nor was Little Maureen anywhere close in the beauty department, but if Draco turned off the lights, he could pretend they were anyone in the world.

He filled a bowl with ice, shoved the bottle of champagne inside and then lit a candle. "Let's get this party started."

"Can you kiss with your lips all twisted like that?" Little Maureen twisted a curl around her finger. "What happened to you?"

"An evil woman took a knife to me." He sat next to her on the sofa. "If you don't want to suffer the same fate she did, you'll stop asking questions." His blood boiled, and he fisted his hands to keep from striking her.

21

"I'm calling to keep you up-to-date on the case," Ingram said on the phone the next morning. "We've had another...incident."

"What happened?" Cassidy waved Colin over.

"The body of a young prostitute was discovered this morning."

"Why do you think her death is related?"

"Written in the dirt next to her body were the words 'pretty is as pretty does'. I know it isn't exactly the same as the others, but the word pretty—"

"We'll be right there." Cassidy grabbed her holstered gun from a peg high on the wall out of the reach of children.

"No, we'll do the investigating. You're in hiding and protective service."

"You can't do this." She flopped onto the sofa. "This is more my case than anyone's. I need to be there when this guy is caught. Bill Carson is armed. If anyone comes snooping around—"

"I gave you a direct order."

"Then call my supervisor." She lunged to her feet and paced. "I'll do this with or without your permission." She waved a hand as Colin opened his mouth to speak. "You know as well as I do that Blake Russell does these things to draw me out. So, let me be there. We won't catch him otherwise. You know it."

Bill Carson grabbed the phone from her hand. "Sir, I would appreciate her leaving this cabin. If this maniac wants her, then having her close to my family puts us in danger." He handed the phone back to Cassidy. "You're welcome." He marched into the kitchen.

"Sir?"

"The man has a point." Ingram sighed. "As much as I hate to say this, go ahead and investigate this lead with MacKenzie. I'll send Smith to watch over the Carsons." He gave her the location of the body and hung up.

Cassidy grinned and fist pumped the air. She might be walking into a trap, but it was better than sitting there wondering what was going on.

She glanced at Rosie who sat looking up at her with intense eyes. The Carson's little boy laughed and threw his arms around the dog's neck. "Stay, Rosie. Guard." It would leave an empty spot in her heart not having her faithful companion with her, but the child could use the protection more.

"Are you sure?" Colin glanced from her to Rosie.

"I'm sure." She heaved a sigh and glanced at the Carson family. "If I don't return for her, take good care of her. She's the best protector you'll ever need." She knelt down and hugged her furry friend. “Be good. I’ll be back by dark.” God willing.

Rosie whined, confused, as Cassidy strolled out the front door.

Without looking back, she climbed into the jeep, grateful for the chance to search for The Dragon rather than wait for him to come to her as she hid in a cabin in the woods.

“You’re either the bravest woman I’ve ever met,” Colin said, “or the dumbest. That dog is the best warning you can have that someone is coming.”

“Which is why I left her behind. If something happened to the children because of my presence, I’d never forgive myself.” She stared at him. “You should understand about not forgiving yourself. You can’t get over something that was an accident. My staying here is not the same thing.”

“Low blow.” He started the ignition and turned the jeep around in the small yard.

“You didn’t have a nightmare last night.”

“I took a pill, and I’m still feeling the effects. They leave me grouchy, so don’t start in on me.”

“All righty then.” She fought a smile and glanced out the window. Perhaps the always grinning Colin wasn’t so perfect after all. How long would his bad mood last? She glanced at her watch.

~

Colin parked next to the yellow crime scene tape in the city’s poorest, and most crime ridden, area. Several gang members and prostitutes stood on the civilian side of the tape and craned their necks to get a look.

"Pardon me." He lifted the tape to let Cassidy through.

Lying on the gravel strewn alley next to a dumpster was the body of a young girl. She didn't look more than fifteen or sixteen. If she was older, she was lying. His heart sank at the loss of such a young life. Red hair fanned out from a face that was more cute than pretty. A short leather skirt barely covered what should be hidden.

He knelt next to her and looked up into the tear-filled eyes of a much older girl. "What's her name?"

"All we know her by is Angel."

"Who was her last trick? Did you know the man?"

She shook her head. "He wasn't a regular." She shuddered. "He was a monster. Handsome on one side, scarred on the other, like Two-Face, the character from the Batman movies. She was wearing jeans when she went with him."

That cinched the fact that Blake Russell was most likely the murderer. Colin pushed to his feet, noticing a young African American man standing off to one side. The man motioned his head, calling Colin closer.

"Do you have information for me?" Colin stepped over the tape.

"That man was here before. A couple of days ago. Me and some of my homies tried to harass him. He pulled out a gun and shot one of us right between the eyes. He's cold. Didn't even flinch when he pulled the trigger, then just walked away."

"Did you see him with the girl?"

"They went into that liquor store for a bottle. I don't know where they went after that. Me and the homies been trying to find him to exact payback, but he's like a ghost."

"He calls himself The Dragon. Stay away from him."

"Dude." The man held up his hands. "We got to pay him back. Just call us the dragon slayers. We'll send you his head."

"Then you'll most likely die." Colin almost threatened to lock the guy up in order to save his life. He glanced at the man's 'homies'. He couldn't lock them all up. He shook his head and headed for the liquor store while Cassidy spoke with the crime scene techs.

A bell jingled over the door when he entered. He glanced up and noted a security camera. "That thing work?"

"Yes, sir. We keep it running on a loop. It doesn't pay to not be vigilant in this neighborhood."

"Do you have the footage from last night?"

"Yep." He motioned Colin to come around the counter. "You can see it all on that monitor."

Colin backed up the video feed until he came to the approximate time Blake had entered the store. The man kept the scarred side of his face away from the camera and grinned, or grimaced, at the young girl at his side. Was it possible he'd slipped up and not noticed the camera?

"How did he seem to you?" He asked the clerk.

“Happy. The girl was giggling. They seemed to be having a good time.”

“She didn’t seem afraid of him?”

“Nope.”

Hmm. Colin glanced at the video again. What had changed? Had she said something to set Blake off? In the video her hair was dark, but outside her hair was red. Was that the trigger? He ejected the tape and slipped it into a paper bag. “Thank you for your cooperation.”

“Any time. Angel was well liked around here.”

Colin headed back out and joined Cassidy. “Any word on her real identity?”

“We’re checking her against missing teens. It will probably take a while. Poor thing.” She scanned the area. “Doesn’t make sense that Blake would go for one so young.”

“Look around. She was the prettiest one here. He probably thought she’d give him the least resistance. The weird thing is, the store clerk said they were laughing while making their purchase. Angel hadn’t seemed frightened of him at all.”

“She said or did something that got her killed. I guess we start knocking on doors. Not the safest thing in this neighborhood.”

“The gang members are out for revenge. I’m sure they’ll help.” If they didn’t kill him before alerting the authorities to his location. In moments like that one, Colin didn’t care if they found the man alive or dead.

“I need some coffee.”

"There's a gas station on the corner. They'll have some. Then we can plan our next step. Did you find any clues around the body?"

"Not a thing, just like all the others." She glanced at her watch. "Are you still grouchy?"

"No. Why?"

"Your bad mood lasted two hours."

"Seriously? You timed it?"

She shrugged and laughed. "It's out of character for you."

She was something else. He grinned and put his arm around her shoulders.

The gang members parted like the Red Sea as the two of them strolled down the sidewalk. A couple of them gave Cassidy appreciative glances, but no one said anything. Their silence gave Colin the creeps. The authorities needed to find The Dragon before the dragon slayers did.

~

Draco removed every trace of Little Maureen from the shoddy apartment. He cleaned the surfaces with bleach, vacuumed the sofa, and tossed the bedding into a pile to be laundered. Her jeans he tossed out the window after dousing them with bleach. They'd find them and link them to the girl, but he didn't care. He'd be long gone by then.

Not that he didn't expect Cassidy and the Scotsman to not figure out he'd killed her, but because it was what he did when he had a victim at his house. Although he hadn't planned on killing the girl, he wanted no traces of her anywhere around.

Once he was certain he'd taken care of anything relating to her, or him, he gathered his things and closed the door. Time to find a new place to live.

He scooted out the back door of the building and headed for his rented Lincoln. Popping the trunk, he tossed his suitcase in the back.

"Hey, Dragon."

He whirled, coming face-to-face with five gang members. "Walk away."

"The cops are looking for you. We told them we'd bring them your head."

"Good luck with that." Draco re-opened the trunk and pulled out a bag. "I'll give you one more chance to walk away."

"Now, that ain't going to happen, Dragon." The leader said his name as if it were a cuss word. "We got to make amends for you killing our friend. Now, it doesn't seem likely that you can shoot all five of us."

Draco pulled a lighter from his pants pocket. "Perhaps not." He set the paper bag on fire and leaped behind the dumpster.

The bag exploded.

Screams filled the air along with the stench of burning flesh.

He sighed and came out of hiding, stepping over the nearest gang member howling on the ground. "You should have listened to me." He gave the man a kick, then climbed into the driver's seat of his car, now showing the effects of the pipe bomb he'd set off. No matter. He'd ditch the car and get another one.

The gang members wouldn't die. The bomb hadn't been powerful enough. But, they would sport a few scars of their own.

He cranked up the radio. Classical music burst from the speakers as he pulled out of the alley. When would the masses learn not to mess with The Dragon? He glanced at the clock in the dashboard. He had thirty minutes before his meeting with his followers.

He spotted the detectives strolling down the sidewalk as if they were on an afternoon excursion. They stepped into the gas station store. Draco parked across the street and watched through the window as the Scotsman bought two coffees.

It would be so easy to pick them off. He thought of the gun in his glove compartment and almost reached for it. No, he had a different end in mind for them. Cassidy needed the opportunity to join him, to share his vision. If not, she would suffer the fate of her mother.

He would wait.

22

An explosion rattled the store window.

"That came from the alley." Cassidy turned to the store clerk. "Where's the back door?"

The young woman pointed. "Should I call the cops?"

"We are the cops!" Colin barged down a short hall and out the back door, Cassidy on his heels.

The five gang members they'd spoken to earlier lay writhing in agony on the ground. The leader clutched a leg missing several layers of skin.

Cassidy placed a call for an ambulance and squatted next to one young man with a stick poking out of his forehead. "Looks like y'all had a run in with The Dragon, and he was breathing fire." She shook her head. "At least everyone here is still breathing. This one barely." She moved the man's hand away from his face. "Don't pull it out. You'll bleed to death."

"I warned you, didn't I?" Colin helped the leader to a sitting position and used the man's belt as a tourniquet.

The young man cursed. "He's bad news for sure."

"So, it was the same guy?"

"Yep. Came out of that apartment complex behind us."

As soon as the ambulance pulled into the alley, Cassidy followed Colin into the apartment complex. A few moments spent with a drowsy manager and they knew which apartment Blake Russell had rented.

"The man always paid cash," the woman said, tightening a stained yellow terry cloth robe around her faded nightgown. "Kept to himself and never gave me a lick of trouble. Not like some of my other tenants."

She led them up the stairs and into an apartment reeking of bleach. "See? The place is spotless. Just like him."

Cassidy cast her an incredulous look. If only the woman knew. "Don't you do background checks on your tenants?"

"I done told you he paid cash. That's all I care about. Y'all let yourselves out." She turned and shuffled back down the stairs.

Cassidy stepped into the sparcely furnished room, snapping gloves onto her hands. "He cleaned it in anticipation of us coming."

"Probably to remove that poor girl's DNA." Colin moved to the window. "He's got a clear view of the street and the prostitutes from here. My guess is...he'd chosen her, whether to die or for company, I don't know."

"He did a lot more than that." Cassidy peered under the sleeper sofa and pulled out a slip of paper torn from a receipt. In girlish scrawl was the name Maureen. "Either she shared my mother's name or that's what he chose to call her."

Blake Russell seemed to be spiralling into decline, especially if he had taken to naming his victims by Cassidy's mother's name. She pushed to her feet and headed to the one other room in the place. The bathroom.

She opened the medicine cabinet to find it empty. Same with the small closet on the other side of the wall. It was as if no one had lived there. Another deadend as far as clues went. Still, they'd have the crime scene investigators scope the place. They knew Blake was their man, but every clue that backed that up made putting him behind bars easier.

"Cassidy." Colin's voice called her from the front room.

She joined him at the front window. A dark Lincoln idled in front of the building. She knew without being able to see through the tinted windows that their killer sat in the driver's seat. She opened the window and leaned out. "Come on up and let's talk."

Her cell phone rang. "Blake?"

"Hello, dear. Have you found the item I left you yet?"

"The slip of paper with my mother's name?"

"No, I didn't know about that. Silly little girl." He chuckled. "She and I got along just fine until she had a slip of the tongue. Very unfortunate."

"What's the item, Blake?"

"I go by Draco now, dear." He sighed. "I thought you were better than this. I hate to make things too easy for you. I need a worthy adversary."

"Come up here and I'll show you how worthy I am." With a bullet in the heart.

"Tsk tsk. When the time is right." Click. The car pulled away from the curb and drove off.

"He said he left us something." Cassidy turned from the window. "There aren't many hiding places here."

"So we look closer. I'll start at this end, you start in the bathroom."

She'd just come from there, but anything was better than standing around guessing. She returned to the small room containing a shower, a toilet, and a pedestal sink. If someone were to hide something, where would they put it? She glanced at the vent overhead. Climbing onto the toilet seat, she removed the screw holding the cover in place. Empty, like everything else.

She jumped down and lifted the lid from the toilet tank. Bingo. Inside was a plastic bag. She pulled it out, shook off the water, then removed the contents and stared at the photos of a smiling, handsome Blake and her mother. They both looked so happy. Were these taken at the same party as the photo Cassidy carried in her pocket?

Had her mother and Blake been an item? Not according to Allison Carson. Rather Blake had wanted her mother and her mother had only tolerated him. As time went on, the more convinced Cassidy was that Blake had had an unhealthy obsession with her mother. An obsession that drove him to kill.

She turned the top photo over. Written in red ink were the words, "Join me or I kill the Scotsman."

~

Colin leaned against the doorjamb and watched as Cassidy's face paled. "What did you find?"

"Pictures and a warning." She handed him the photos. "He's coming after you."

"I've been expecting him to. He won't catch me unawares."

Her eyes glistened. "Being my partner could get you killed."

"Hazard of the job." He held out his hand. "Come on. Let's meet with Ingram, tell him what we have, and head back up the mountain. Don't worry about me."

He could tell his words didn't soothe her. She would worry, because that's who she was. She'd grown to care for him, despite her struggles to the contrary, and this note would only make her worry more.

Slipping her hand into his, she allowed him to pull her to her feet and out of the room. He gathered her in his arms, breathing deep of her scent, only for a moment, then released her. He tilted her face to his. "I'll be fine. No dragon is going to end me." He grinned, fighting back the urge to kiss her. With a woman as opposed to romantic entanglements as Cassidy, it was best to let her make the first move. “I’m glad you aren’t considering the contrary.”

“Which is?” Her voice shook.

“Joining the family business.”

She choked back a laugh. “This is serious.”

“We’ve known from the beginning the risks of this job.” He chucked her on the chin. “Chin up, Bull Dog. We’ve a killer to catch.”

“Don’t call me that.” She stepped back, her gaze locked on his. “If something were to happen—”

“We’ll deal with it when and if.” He moved out of the apartment, pulling the door closed after Cassidy. The crime scene techs would come here when they finished with the alley.

The message on the photo bothered him, he wouldn’t lie. Draco the dragon stayed one step ahead of them all the time. The only thing going for Colin was instincts and a desire to live. It would have to be enough.

They met Ingram in the alley. Cassidy handed him the baggie and photos. “This is why I can’t hide. The clues are for me to find.”

“You’ve made your point.” Ingram dropped the evidence into a bag. “The toilet, you say? Doubt there’s anything on it after being in the water.”

“We didn’t find a hair in the place. Just a slip of paper with the name Maureen.” Colin nodded for Cassidy to hand it over. “We’re heading back up the mountain to try and come up with another plan to draw this perp out.”

"Good luck," Ingram said. "We're batting zero. If you're a praying man, tell the big guy upstairs we could use a break"

Colin nodded and placed his hand on the small of Cassidy's back. They made their way back to the jeep, ignoring the curious looks of the bystanders. Maybe the gang's pals would help bring The Dragon down.

"I don't want to go back to the mountain," Cassidy said. "Blake may not know where the cabin is, and I want him to come to me."

"Your house? What about backup?"

"Call Ingram and tell him where we're going. We've got the security system. We'll know Blake is there the moment he steps foot on my property."

He didn't like it. Not a bit. "It's too dangerous."

"I'm not going to have a war at the cabin where a baby and innocent people are. You should understand how painful it is to be the cause of an innocent's death."

He knew all too well. "This is different. I pulled the trigger that killed that woman."

"It'll feel the same to me if one of the Carsons is hit." She gave him a sharp look. "You can't stay awake forever. The moment you fall asleep, I'll be in the jeep and headed home."

"Fine." He whipped the steering wheel and turned the jeep around.

~

"Where are they going?" Mary whispered, narrowing her eyes as the jeep swung and drove in the opposite direction of the mountain cabin. Surely they weren't headed back to town. Bringing down Draco's nemesis would be much harder under the watchful eyes of nosy neighbors. She cursed and followed.

Sure enough, less than an hour later, the two cops pulled into the female's driveway. Minus the dog, which would be a huge plus when Mary needed to break in. She needed to find a way through the security system. There were bound to be cameras and alarms.

No worries. She was a smart woman, one of the most intelligent she knew. The only thing she had over her step-sisters. She smiled. Former step-sisters.

She'd find a way in. If not, she'd simply ring the front doorbell and have them invite her in. Draco would be amazed at her prowess, her ingenuity, her bravery, her *worth*. He might even make her his second-in-command.

A thrill shot through her. She had found her new purpose. To become the most important person in Draco's life. He would love her. After all, the man wouldn't care that she was plain. He, himself, was scarred. No, they'd become the most formidable duo in the history of the world.

She laughed and drove past the house. Life couldn't be better for Mary Jones.

Before returning to her motel room, she stopped for fast food burgers. The largest they had. She was celebrating her good fortune, after all.

In her room, she set the food on the round table for two and headed for the bathroom to change into a flannel nightgown and a terry robe. Once she and

Draco became an item, she'd need something more…feminine. Her face heated at the thought. She'd bet he was a generous lover. Not rough and hurtful like her father had been.

Some would say the hate inside Mary was caused by life. She knew it was because she was being fashioned into someone worthy of Draco. Unless she could overcome the tragedies of her past, she couldn't welcome the future that promised to be more than she'd ever dreamed.

She plopped across the bed and opened the food bag. After taking a bite of the greasy burger, she dialed the number to the man she loved.

"Why are you calling, Mary?" His voice sent her stomach fluttering. "I thought we discussed you moving on now."

"I have the grandest plans, too. Oh, Draco, you'll be so proud of me."

23

Mary entered the nearest pawn shop and leaned over the counter, giving the man a healthy view of her bosom. She needed a few things, had little funds, and would do anything for Draco, even cheapen herself.

She pointed at an assault rifle hanging on the wall. "I want that and several boxes of ammo." She grinned.

"Going hunting?" The man's gaze flickered over her shoulder, then back to her face.

"Something like that." Her smile faded as she glanced back at the television. The local news station was showing the weather. Hot and muggy today. Nothing that compelling or strange enough to warrant the clerk's rapt attention.

The clerk set the rifle and ammo on the counter. "I'll need you to fill out some paperwork."

"Sure." She lifted the rifle and quickly loaded it as he turned to get the forms. When his hand hovered under the counter, she fired. "I wish you wouldn't have done that."

She glance at the television again and saw her face plastered on the screen. She cursed, grabbed the rest of the ammo and darted outside. Seconds later she sped away from the pawn shop.

~

As had become her norm, Cassidy stood in front of the caseboard in her basement, cup of coffee in hand, and tried to reconstruct the board she'd set up at the cabin and make sense out of the seemingly random clues. Photos and red lines connecting them filled the space. She needed the other board back asap.

"Let's go." Colin came half way down the stairs. "Ingram called. Got an alert from a pawn shop seconds after Mary Jones's photo was shown on the local news station."

Cassidy bounded up the stairs and set her mug in the sink before grabbing her weapon and following Colin out the door. They sped toward the pawn shop, arriving before Ingram was out of his car.

"First responders report a body inside," he said. "My guess is…she caught him pressing the alarm, shot, and fled."

They'd lost her again. Cassidy scanned the area. The same rundown part of town they'd been in yesterday with the same crowd of onlookers. "I'll question the crowd. See if anyone saw anything."

A homeless man got to his feet as Cassidy passed. "I saw what happened." His words slurred and he breathed a wave of whiskey fumes across her face. "Woman went in, I heard a gunshot, and she ran back out with a rifle and got into a rusty Impala."

Cassidy pulled Mary's photo from her bag. "Was it this woman?"

"Yep." He held out his hand and wiggled his fingers. "Don't leave me hanging."

She sighed and fished a twenty dollar bill from her pocket. "Thank you for the information. Which direction did she flee?"

"That way." He pointed the way she and Colin had come.

They'd passed her. She'd be long gone by now.

"We missed her," she said standing next to Colin. "Probably passed her on the highway, but I have an affirmative ID."

A muscle ticked in his jaw. "One step ahead, again, and we have absolutely nothing to go on other than the fact it was definitely her."

"There's also been no sign of the Dragon." Ingram shook his head. "We viewed the store's video footage. Mary Jones entered alone and left alone. The clerk was dead when we arrived."

"Do you think she's acting alone now?" Cassidy glanced between the two men. "Stealing a gun doesn't seem to be Blake Russell's style. What if, now that she's murdered her sisters, she feels she needs to do something more?"

"That's a big what if," Ingram said.

"Remember, these people are mentally unstable. Just because it doesn't mean anything to us, it could make perfect sense to them."

"What warrants this assumption?"

She glanced at Colin and smiled. "I've learned a bit about trusting my instincts from Colin."

"No better person to learn from. This man is the best." Ingram clapped him on the shoulder. "We're going to finish up here. You two head back to the house and study that board. Find what we're missing."

"What we're missing is the killer and my caseboard," Cassidy mumbled. "I stare at that board every morning and every evening. I left it at the cabin."

"We'll get it so you can stare some more." Ingram marched away.

"Bossy man." She exhaled sharply through her nose and fished her cell phone from her pocket. She pressed redial on the last number Blake called her from, not expecting him to answer. When he did, she waved Colin over and mouthed who was on the other end of the line.

"Hello, dear. Now, I need to get a new phone."

"I didn't really expect you to answer." Her eyes widened. "I have a question for you."

"I might have an answer, but make it quick. I don't want you trying to pinpoint my location. I'll hang up in twenty-five seconds."

"Why did Mary steal a gun and shoot a pawnstore clerk? Were you behind that?"

"Definitely not. I have more finesse. Beware of her." Click.

~

"What did he say?" Colin snapped his fingers to get Ingram's attention.

"That he isn't behind Mary's actions this morning and for me to beware."

"She's coming after you." Colin yanked open the door to the jeep and shoved her inside. A crazy woman after Cassidy and a maniac after him. Things were on a downhill slide for sure.

"What are you doing?"

"Saving you." He turned to Ingram. "We'll call if we find out anything." He got into the driver's seat and sped away.

"Don't manhandle me, Colin." Cassidy crossed her arms. "Weren't you the one who said we were aware of the dangers when we took this job? I don't need to be shuffled off home like a wayward teenager."

He cut her a sideways glance. "Have you forgotten one of my duties is to protect you? I wish you hadn't left the dog behind. You don't make it easy, and I can use all the help I can get."

"We'll get her back when this is all over." She lifted her chin and turned away. "I can protect myself."

"Have you forgot who we're dealing with?"

"Nope." She still wouldn't look at him.

"Are you mad at me?" He frowned.

"No, maybe, yes. A little."

"Why?"

She turned and glared. "Everything is going to come to a boil. One of us, or both, may not make it out alive. If Blake wants me to join his so-called murder group, you're in the way. He'll eliminate anything that keeps me from fulfilling his diabolical plan."

"I've told you not to worry about me." Why couldn't she understand he wasn't going anywhere? That sticking close to her was all the plan he had? "I'm good at my job, Cassidy."

"So am I." High spots of color appeared in her cheeks.

"Then, let's work together. This has nothing to do with whether me, or Ingram, think you incapable. It's time for you to get the chip off your shoulder and accept the fact you are no longer a lone wolf."

Her eyes glittered. She started to say something, then clamped her lips together and turned away.

So be it. Angry and alive was better than happy and dead. The only problem he could see was in her attempts to keep him from harm, she might put hers in the bullseye. He couldn't let that happen.

He reached over to take her hand, but she pulled away, clasping her hands in her lap. He sighed and pulled into her driveway. For the first time since meeting her, he didn't open the door for her. Instead, he marched up the steps and onto the porch to punch in the code for the alarm. No blinking red light told him the alarm was set. Had they left in such a hurry that morning they'd forgotten? Possible, but he wasn't taking any chances.

"What's wrong?" Cassidy stepped to his side.

"The alarm isn't set."

"That's my fault. I left behind you this morning. I must have forgotten."

He shot her a sharp look and pulled his weapon from his holster. "Irresponsible."

"I'm not used to being a prisoner in my own home. I'll go in first."

He blocked her path. "No."

Pushing the door open, he peered inside. Everything appeared normal. Cassidy's OCD nature of everything in its place didn't look disturbed. He waved her in. "You've got to be more careful. Follow me as we check each room, even the basement."

She nodded. "I'm sorry."

They checked each room and found nothing out of place. With each search, Colin's frustration grew. He understood how they forgot to set the alarm, but that mistake could have been disastrous.

"Are you hungry?" Cassidy set her gun on the kitchen table. "I could order a pizza."

"Not mad anymore?"

She sighed. "We all make mistakes. I apologize for my rudeness. You're right. I have a chip on my shoulder the size of Mount Everest. It's grown over the years as I've fought to prove my worth in law enforcement." She met his gaze. "I know I'm a good detective. The human side of me wants kudos, I guess."

"I'll give you all the praise you need." He grinned. "A pizza sounds great. Meat lovers, please." He pulled out a kitchen chair and stared toward the kitchen window. The curtains were open a little, moving in a soft breeze. "Did you leave that open?"

"No, I wouldn't have." She moved to close the window and draw the curtains. "Maybe I'm losing my mind." After closing the curtains, she pulled a bottle of red wine from the cupboard. "Want a glass?"

"After what almost happened the last time we drank? No, thanks." Not to mention the fact a killer wanted Cassidy and had warned her about one of his minions. "We need to stay alert."

She put the bottle back on the shelf. "Do you think she'll come tonight?"

"I do." He folded his hands on the table. "The alarm should give us warning, though. I know it's dangerous, but we're sleeping together tonight." Not that he had any intentions of closing his eyes. He didn't need the nightmares or to lose his focus. "I'll take the floor next to the bed. Ingram said all the repairs were made to the wall."

"I'll gather some blankets and pillows." She placed a call for pizza and headed down the hall.

Colin placed his chair to where he could see her. "Don't take those upstairs without me."

"The alarm is set. I'm perfectly safe."

"You don't leave my sight, understand?"

She dropped the bedding on the bottom step. "Am I allowed to use the restroom?"

"The powder room downstairs." Irritable or not, he wasn't going to relent on her staying in sight. Blake Russell had shown he possessed skills far surpassing most of the criminals Colin had dealt with in his career. He wasn't taking any chances. Not only was it his job, but he had come to care for her more than he'd thought possible.

The fiery red-headed detective had wormed her way into his heart and set up roots. He wouldn't survive if he failed to keep her safe. If he'd known leaving Scotland would result in him falling in love, he wasn't sure he would have left. Romance brought entanglements into a law enforcement partnership that muddied the waters and increased risk.

"If not wine, then coffee," Cassidy said exiting the powder room and entering the kitchen. "It's going to be a long sleepless night."

The doorbell rang.

Colin pushed to his feet. "I'll get it."

"There's money in the jar on the table."

"My treat." He turned off the alarm and, after verifying the pizza delivery boy stood there, opened the door.

Stepping into sight, gun pointed at the center of his forehead, was Mary Jones.

24

"Hello, handsome." Mary stepped forward, keeping the gun aimed at his head. "Pizza boy, sit in the corner and be good. Sorry you dropped your joint when I walked up. Smoking that weed is bad for you anyway.

"Now, Handsome, step back nice and slow." When he did, she kicked the door closed. "So nice of you to answer the door."

"I was only expecting pizza." Colin gave her the crooked grin that always worked for him with women.

"Oh, you're a charmer, for sure. It won't work, though." Not returning his smile, she cocked her head to the side. "A shame you'll be dead soon. You and the woman, probably the boy, too."

Cassidy lunged through the doorway her gun aimed at Mary. "Put it down."

"Follow your advice or pretty boy dies right now. Nice and slow. I'll do it. First one leg, then the other. Maybe a graze along one gorgeous cheek." A slow smile spread across her face. “Drop the gun and kick it to me, that’s a good girl.”

Cassidy’s features hardened as she followed the woman’s directions.

“All three of you into the living room and strip to your undies. Remove your socks and shoes.” Mary watched as they stripped, then laughed. “For a beauty, your lingerie leaves something to be desired.”

Colin cut a sideways glance at Cassidy’s simple white bra and panties. She was beautiful in her simplicity, and he hoped he’d have a chance to tell her so and elicit a blush from her again.

He glanced around for a weapon. The woman was smart in making him and Cassidy as vulnerable as possible. Cassidy’s sparcely decorated home left little for him to use. The floor lamp would be too unwieldy. He’d have to watch for an opportunity to take her down by brute force.

As the delivery boy’s baggy jeans dropped to the floor, Colin spotted the corner of a cell phone peeking from the pocket. If he could get to it—

“Handsome, sit in that chair where I can see you. Detective Monroe and Pizza Boy sit on the sofa.” Mary leaned against the doorjamb. “Is everyone comfy?”

“My name is Danny.” The delivery boy scowled. “If this is a robbery, I only carry twenty dollars on me.”

“Aren’t you cute.” Mary slapped his pimpled cheek. “No more talking. I only have questions for one person in this room and that’s the red-headed beauty.” She squatted in front of Cassidy. “I don’t understand something. Draco hates beautiful people. Why the fixation on you?"

Cassidy laughed. "Didn't he tell you? He's my father."

Mary paled. "Impossible. He would have told me something that important."

"It seems Bla...Draco has a few secrets."

Mary pushed to her feet and paced, keeping the gun trained on those sitting. "This muddles things."

If Colin could distract her a bit more, get her to lower the gun... He shifted, drawing her attention.

"Huh-uh, pretty boy. Stay still. I can see the thoughts in your mind."

If she really could read his mind, she'd drop dead from the violence of his thoughts. Colin glanced at Cassidy. Rather than fear, he saw determination on her face. *That's my girl*. The poor boy didn't know whether to exist in a pot-induced haze or wet himself.

Mary resumed her pacing. "It makes sense, really. Draco's almost protective attitude toward you." She leaned close enough to Cassidy to force her to lean back. "I came here to kill you. I guess I can't do that to the woman who will one day be my stepdaughter. Now, how to get you to Draco. He'll be so pleased, he's bound to give me anything I want. The desire of my heart will soon be mine."

While she was focused on Cassidy, Colin dove for the cell phone. He managed to punch in Ingram's number and hit speaker before the bullet slammed into his side. The second shot took him high in the thigh.

~

"Stop!" Cassidy scrambled toward him, grabbing their discarded clothes to help staunch the bleeding. "Stay with me, Colin."

"Get up, Detective." Mary rapped her on the shoulder with the revolver. "He's going to bleed to death before help can get here." She cursed as the delivery boy raced through the kitchen.

The slamming of the backdoor told Cassidy the boy made it out. "I won't leave him. You'll have to shoot me, too." Tears burned her throat as Colin's blood soaked into her carpet. Mary knew she couldn't shoot Cassidy. Not unless she wanted to incur Blake's wrath.

The other woman peered through the curtains. "Cops will be here any minute. You might die in a hail of bullets. Are you afraid, Detective?"

Only of Colin dying. "No."

"So brave. Just like your father." Mary pulled out her cell phone. "Draco, I have a dilemma…well, I told you I was going to do something for you…I'm here with your daughter. I didn't know she was your daughter, of course, is she? Really? What a pity. I've shot the Scot. The cops are coming. How do I get out of here with her?" Tears pooled in Mary's eyes, and then ran down her round cheeks. "That's really what you want me to do? I love you…all right, Draco. See you on the other side. Please don't keep me waiting too long."

Mary sighed, the sound as lonely and mournful as anything Cassidy had ever heard. Then, the woman turned the gun on herself and pulled the trigger. Blood and brain matter sprayed the wall behind her. Her eyes widened, then she toppled over. Still.

Shocked, Cassidy couldn't move for a moment. Then, realizing the severity of Colin's wounds, and the fact the danger for her had passed, she darted for the front door and yanked it open as Ingram and an ambulance roared onto her driveway. "Hurry!"

Ingram gave Cassidy a wide-eyed look at her in her underwear as he rushed past her. The paramedics were a bit more professional. They didn't spare her so much as a peek. While they worked on Colin, she donned her sweat pants and tee shirt then slid her feet into flip-flops.

"Can you save him? Please save him." She stepped close as they lifted him onto a gurney. "Colin, can you hear me?" She trotted after the medics, determined to ride in the ambulance. She hoisted herself inside before anyone could say no and took Colin's hand in hers.

This was her fault. For years, she'd managed to not have a partner because of the small size of Clear Springs's population. Now, after being forced into having her second one, she was close to losing him. Not only that he was her partner, but she loved him. Something she'd vowed never to do.

The drive to the hospital seemed to take hours when in actuality it took ten minutes. Cassidy stepped aside as the paramedics rushed Colin inside. A receptionist told her to wait in the waiting room and the doctor would notify her when he had something to report.

Cassidy had never felt more alone in her life. She plopped into a vinyl chair and stared at the ceiling, counting the tiles. She quit when she got to 307. What was taking so long?

A man in blue scrubs walked toward her. She leaped to her feet only to watch as he passed her and approached an older woman. Cassidy sighed and fell back into her chair.

"No news?" Ingram sat next to her.

"None. It's only been an hour." She stared at the ceiling again.

"Tell me what happened at your place."

"We ordered pizza. She was hiding around the corner, using the delivery boy as a shield. When Colin answered the doorbell, she forced the delivery boy inside, made us strip, and had every intention of killing all three of us until she found out I was Blake Russell's daughter. Then, she called him and shot herself. I think he told her to."

"Hmm." Ingram jotted notes on a small notebook. "The delivery boy is fine. He's home with his folks. Mary died immediately. Your house is...smelly." He gave her a wry grin. "I'll send someone over to clean it. Keep your chin up. It'll take more than a crazy woman to kill MacKenzie."

She nodded. It would be her that killed him. Whether by accident or through someone else, she would be at blame. "I hope so."

Two hours later, the doctor came down the long hallway. "Detective Monroe? I'm Doctor Savalli."

Cassidy jumped to her feet. "Is he all right?"

"He's going to be fine. A few months of physical therapy due to the shot to the leg, but he's going to be as good as new."

Relief flooded through her so strongly, her knees weakened. She grabbed the doctor's arm for support. "May I see him?"

"He's unconscious, but yes, you may go in." He directed her to Colin's room.

She hurried to his room and stared down at a stranger. The strong, vibrant man was hidden by tubes and pale skin. "I'm so sorry, Colin." She let the tears she'd been holding in fall down her cheeks. She leaned forward and placed a kiss on his lips. "I can't do this. I love you. Goodbye, sweetheart."

She straightened, and taking a deep breath, left Colin and any hopes for a future with him behind.

The End of volume 1

For more of Cassidy and Colin as they work on capturing the elusive Draco, stayed tuned for book 2, coming Spring 2016. **Will Colin forgive Cassidy for leaving him behind and moving to another town?**

ABOUT THE AUTHOR

Multi-published and Amazon Best-Selling author Cynthia Hickey had three cozy mysteries and two novellas published through Barbour Publishing. Her first mystery, Fudge-Laced Felonies, won first place in the inspirational category of the Great Expectations contest in 2007. Her third cozy, Chocolate-Covered Crime, received a four-star review from Romantic Times. All three cozies have been re-released as ebooks through the MacGregor Literary Agency, along with a new cozy series, all of which stay in the top 50 of Amazon's ebooks for their genre. She had several historical romances release in 2013, 2014, 2015 through Harlequin's Heartsong Presents, and has sold half a million copies of her works. She has taught a Continuing Education class at the 2015 American Christian Fiction Writers conference. She is active on FB, twitter, and Goodreads, and is a contributor to Cozy Mystery Magazine blog and Suspense Sisters blog. Her and her husband run the small press, Forget Me Not Romances, which includes some of the CBA's well-known authors. She lives in Arizona with her husband, one of their seven children, two dogs, two cats, three box turtles, and two Sulcata tortoises. She has seven grandchildren who keep her busy and tell everyone they know that "Nana is a writer". Visit her website at www.cynthiahickey.com

Enjoy other books by Cynthia Hickey

Nosy Neighbor Series

Anything For A Mystery, Book 1

A Killer Plot, Book 2

Skin Care Can Be Murder, Book 3

Death By Baking, Book 4

Jogging Is Bad For Your Health, Book 5

Poison Bubbles, Book 6

A Good Party Can Kill You, Book 7 (Final)

Christmas with Stormi Nelson

The Summer Meadows Series

Fudge-Laced Felonies, Book 1

Candy-Coated Secrets, Book 2

Chocolate-Covered Crime, Book 3

Maui Macadamia Madness, Book 4

All four novels in one collection

The River Valley Mystery Series

Deadly Neighbors, Book 1

Advance Notice, Book 2

The Librarian's Last Chapter, Book 3

All three novels in one collection

See Cynthia's other books at www.cynthiahickey.com

Historical Romances

Taming the Sheriff

Finding Love the Harvey Girl Way

Cooking With Love

Guiding With Love

Serving With Love

Warring With Love

All 4 in 1

A Wild Horse Pass Novel

They Call Her Mrs. Sheriff, book 1 (A Western Romance)

Finding Love in Disaster

The Rancher's Dilemma

The Teacher's Rescue

Woman of courage Series

A Love For Delicious

Ruth's Redemption

Charity's Gold Rush

Mountain Redemption

Woman of Courage series (all four books)

Short Story Westerns

Desert Rose

Desert Lilly

Desert Belle

Desert Daisy

Flowers of the Desert 4 in 1

Romantic Suspense

Overcoming Evil series

Mistaken Assassin

Captured Innocence

Mountain of Fear

Exposure at Sea

A Secret to Die for

Collision Course

Romantic Suspense of 5 books in 1

Contemporary

Romance in Paradise

Maui Magic

Sunset Kisses

Deep Sea Love

3 in 1

Finding a Way Home

Christmas

Handcarved Christmas

Curtain Calls and Christmas Wishes

Christmas Gold

A Christmas Stamp

The Red Hat's Club (Contemporary novellas)

Finally

Suddenly

Surprisingly

The Red Hat's Club 3 – in 1

Made in the USA
San Bernardino, CA
08 March 2016